FLANNEL GOWNS AND GRANNY PANTIES

Flannel Gowns and Granny Panties

John Legget Jones

Publisher's note: This is a work of fiction. Names, characters, places, and incidents either are the product of the author's imagination or are used fictitiously. Any resemblance to actual events, locales, or persons, living or dead, is entirely coincidental.

Printed in the United States of America
Edited, formatted, and interior design by Kristen Corrects, Inc.
Cover art design by Laura Duffy Design

First edition published 2016
10 9 8 7 6 5 4 3 2 1

Jones, John Legget
Flannel gowns and granny panties / John Legget Jones
p. cm.
ISBN-13: 9780997329612
ISBN-10: 0997329610

Author website – www.johnleggetjones.com

CHAPTER 1

My name is Ed Sterling and I'm the author of the book *Flannel Gowns and Granny Panties*. I know you have heard my story, everybody has. I was the punchline on TV gossip and late night comedy shows for weeks. You may think you know all about me but before you write me off as the village idiot, let me tell you my story.

I was born and raised in Lake Forest, Illinois, an upper-income community north of Chicago. An only child, I had wonderful parents and a nice life with a big house, new cars, and expensive vacations.

My father is a prominent psychologist with a successful practice specializing in marriage counseling. He told me as I grew up that helping keep couples together was a great, personally rewarding job. I believed him. All I ever wanted to be was a marriage counselor. When I was a little kid, I pretended to be a counselor to my toys. Sure, along the way, I also wanted to be a Cubs baseball player and a police officer. However, I always came back to wanting to be a counselor. I admired what my father did. He became a marriage counselor to help people and he engrained that in me.

My plan was to follow his example so I went to the same schools he did. I got my undergraduate degree in psychology from Northwestern then went to the University of Chicago for my master's degree and doctorate in psychology.

What I learned quickly when I started my practice was that being a marriage counselor was more work than I expected. You meet with a couple and listen for hours about their lives. In the privacy of a counselor's office, people open up and tell you their deepest secrets. You learn everything about a couple including things you don't want to know and can't easily forget. You try to find the underlying causes of the issues in a marriage then give the couple the best advice you can, but guess what happens: They ignore your advice and the marriage eventually ends. My success rate in keeping couples together was about one in four. It was terribly depressing.

I thought I must be bad at my job so I checked around with other marriage counselors. The good ones were no more successful. Knowing this should have made me feel better, but it didn't. I talked to my father about it and was surprised to find he was doing about the same. However, there was a difference between us. He never gave up on a couple and was always optimistic that he could help them. Not me—I would give up on a couple if I thought they couldn't work it out. I told some couples they were never going to work through their issues. Some appreciated it and others didn't. One guy took a swing at me when I told him. (For the record, the couple divorced later after seeing another counselor for two years.)

After being in business for eight years, I was thinking about quitting. I loved my job when I helped make a marriage work and I died a little each time when one failed. In order to stay sane, I had to improve my success rate or find a new career. I spent a lot of time thinking about how I could improve. I reviewed my case files with my father and other marriage counselors to determine if I was doing anything wrong, but I wasn't.

At a conference, I asked an associate about his practice. I learned he had a much higher success rate and I asked him what he did differently. He said his success rate went up when he became more selective on the couples he counseled. He said he wouldn't counsel a couple if he felt they wouldn't stay together. I asked him how he decided who he would counsel. He said it was his gut feeling on whether he thought the couple had any chance of staying together.

I decided to develop a test to help me decide which couples I would counsel. I wanted to ask the right questions and then quickly judge if the couple would make it. If they passed my test, then we would work on the marriage together. If not, I would tell them they should go somewhere else.

Yeah, I know what you're thinking. *What kind of counselor is this guy?* If you think I'm a quick-fix guy, you're right, I am. I'm like every other American. I have a problem: fix it for me now, not tomorrow. I saw my practice in the same way. Diagnose quickly if the couple can make it; if not, move on.

Now that you have a little background, I can tell you my story. I will start with how I developed the test.

CHAPTER 2

When I started to develop my test, I struggled. I asked the wrong questions as well as too many questions. I found myself buried in information and still couldn't determine which couples I should help. For months, I made no progress.

One weekend, I was reading an article in a men's health magazine and there was a quiz rating how healthy you were. In the test, each answer received a score. At the end, there was a total score. A high score meant you were in good health. I liked the test's style and felt it could be adapted for what I needed.

I now had a test method but no questions to use. I spent a lot of time trying to come up with the right questions to ask. I tested my questions on successful couples I had worked with. Slowly, I came up with a test that worked. Once I started using it, my success rate zoomed. I started saving nine out of ten marriages. The couples were happy and I started getting more referrals than I could handle.

I use the test when a couple first comes to my office. As I get to know them, I ask the questions without letting the couple know what I'm doing. You will read my questions soon and you may think my questions are sexist. You're right—the test focuses on the male. There is a reason I concentrate on the man because in my experience the men are responsible for most issues in a marriage. The key word is "most," not "all." Women do dumb things as well but in what I've seen in my practice, men screw up much more.

In their relationships with their wives, men tend to be inconsiderate, rude, and lazy. In far too many of my marriage counseling cases, the man doesn't recognize when he has a woman he should try his best to hold on to. My test tries to help the man see that.

I'd suggest women not read the next section. Here are the questions:

1. Does your wife work? Yes – Add 5 points
2. Is her income between:
    a. $25,000 to $50,000 – Add 1 point
    b. $50,000 to $75,000 – Add 2 points
    c. $75,000 to $100,000 – Add 3 points
    d. $100,000 or more – Add 4 points
3. Does she cook?
    a. No – Subtract 3 points
    b. Yes – Add 3 points. Is she a good cook? Yes – Add 3 more points
4. Does your wife clean the house?
    a. No – Subtract 3 points
    b. Occasionally – Subtract 1 point
    c. Yes but she complains about it – Add 2 points
    d. Yes and she does a decent job – Add 3 points
    e. Yes and she does a good job – Add 5 points
5. How would you rate your wife's intelligence: (Pick one)
    a. Smart – Add 5 points
    b. Average - Add 2 points
    c. Below average – Subtract 1 point
    d. Way below average – Subtract 3 points
6. How would people rate your wife's personality? (Pick up to two)
    a. Fun and outgoing – Add 3 points
    b. Pleasant to be with - Add 2 points
    c. Friendly – Add 2 points
    d. Reserved and quiet – Add 1 point
    e. Bossy or dominating – Subtract 2 points

   f. Odd or quirky – Subtract 2 points
   g. Irritating – Subtract 3 points
   h. Mean – Subtract 4 points
   i. Bad temper – Subtract 4 points

7. How would other men rate your wife's appearance: (Pick one)
   a. Ugly – Subtract 3 points
   b. Plain – Subtract 1 point
   c. Average – Add 1 point
   d. Attractive – Add 3 points
   e. Smoking hot – Add 5 points
8. Do you: (Pick one)
   a. Avoid being with her – Subtract 3 points
   b. Tolerate being with her – Subtract 2 points
   c. Could be with her or not – Subtract 1 point
   d. Like being with her – Add 3 points
   e. Love being with her – Add 5 points
9. Does she drink:
   a. Not at all or only socially – Add 3 points
   b. Occasionally – Add 1 point
   c. Often but not to excess – Subtract 1 point
   d. Often and to excess – Subtract 3 points
   e. She is an alcoholic – Subtract 10 points
10. Does she use drugs?
    a. Never – Add 3 points
    b. Occasionally – Subtract 2 points
    c. Often and to excess – Subtract 3 points
    d. She is addicted to a drug – Subtract 10 points
11. Does she use marijuana?
    a. Never – Add 3 points
    b. Occasionally – Subtract 1 point
    c. Often and to excess – Subtract 2 points
    d. Far too much – Subtract 5 points
12. Does she enjoy the sports you like? Yes – add 5 points

13. Does she watch pro wrestling? Yes – Subtract 5 points
14. Does she consider pro wrestling a real sport? Yes – Subtract 5 points
15. Does she consider roller derby a real sport? Yes – Subtract 3 points
16. Does she have more than three pets? Yes – Subtract 5 points
    a. Does she have a talking parrot? Yes – Subtract 5 points
    b. Does she allow the pet or pets to sleep in your bed? Yes – Subtract 5 points
17. Does your wife eat in bed? Yes – Subtract 5 points
18. Does your wife want to leave the television on while you are making love? Yes – Subtract 5 points
19. Does she use the bathroom while you are in it? Yes – Subtract 5 points
20. Does she own a sexy nightgown? Yes – Add 1 point
21. Does she wear a sexy nightgown often? Yes – Add 3 points
22. Does she wear pajamas or sweatpants on a regular basis outside of the home when you are with her? Yes – Subtract 5 points
    a. Do the sweatpants have a logo or words across the backside? Yes – Subtract 3 points
23. Does she wear camo on a night out with you? Yes – Subtract 5 points
24. Does she wear long flannel gowns on a regular basis? Yes – Subtract 5 points
25. Does she wear granny panties on a regular basis? (Granny panties are cotton panties that cover a woman's bottom and pull up to the waist.) Yes – Subtract 5 points
26. If you go away on a romantic weekend or you are having a romantic evening, does she wear granny panties or a flannel gown to bed?
    a. Yes for the granny panties – Subtract 10 points
    b. Yes for the flannel gown – Subtract 5 points

Here is the scorecard:

30 points or above – I help the man see that the woman is an angel and he should do whatever he has to do to keep her.
20 to 29 points – I tell the couple there are issues to work on but cheer up, you can work through them.
15 to 19 points – I tell the couple the relationship will be difficult to fix.
6 to 14 points – I tell the couple I can't help them.
0 to 5 points – I tell the couple I can't help them and I tell the man to consider getting a protective order.
Less than 0 – I tell the man to run for his life.

The rest of this chapter is for a female reader.

If you are female, you are probably asking yourself, *Where is the test for the man?* I'm sure you could think of many questions. Such as, if the man wears tightie whities, he should get points off. Another one could be a man should get points off if he has a gigantic beer belly or hair all over his body. I included questions like these to score the man in early versions of the test. However, having these questions didn't improve my success rate so I dropped them.

Now I ask only two questions to the woman:

1. Do you want to stay in this relationship?
2. If you may need to make some changes to keep the relationship, will you?

If she says yes to both then I'm willing to work with her. A woman will stay with a man who is awful if she loves him. Women are strong and forgiving. I admire that.

I will start my story three years after developing the test. My wife and I were having an anniversary dinner for my parents at our home in Lake Forest on a Friday evening. That night, my life started to unravel.

CHAPTER 3

"Eddie, your parents will be here in twenty minutes. You need to get ready," said Pam as she entered the master bedroom. "Remember tomorrow evening, we are going to a dinner meeting in downtown Chicago."

"Yes, I remember."

"I'm going to get the girls ready," she said.

"I need a kiss before you leave." I wrapped a towel around me and walked over to her and kissed her. "Maybe we can take a few minutes and I can have a quick sample."

"No you don't! I know how long your samples take. You'll mess up my hair. We don't have the time now!"

"What if I promise not to mess up your hair?"

"No, you always mess up my hair! After the party we'll have time."

"You know one of my key rules in my practice is a couple should be spontaneous in their affection."

"Yeah right! Somehow you always bring up the rules you like whenever you want something. Whenever I need you to take out the trash, you tell me we need to share in household tasks!"

I smiled and said, "It's true I do say that. I'm suggesting you should share now. I'm more than willing to help you with this particular task."

She laughed. "This is the only task you're always willing to help me with. I promise we will have time later."

"I'll remember that."

"You always do!"

Pam kissed me and left to get the girls ready. I watched her leave and thought she was prettier now than when we married. Some women blossom as they age, and Pam has. I have always noticed that wherever we go, she turns men's heads.

In my opinion, I married the best woman in the world. Pam is a successful tax partner in a large accounting firm, an excellent mother, and she is smoking hot! I don't mean pretty, but drop-your-jaw Hollywood pretty.

Pam was well on her way to an executive position before we met. The way she managed to become a partner and have two girls is a great story of hard work and dedication. She manages her time better than anyone I have ever met. Pam hired a nanny for the girls who is part of our family now. Rebecca is twenty-three; she is from England and my girls adore her. She lives in an apartment over our garage. Pam and Rebecca coordinate the girls' schedules so that they are kept busy with school, soccer, and music lessons but still have plenty of time to play.

For all her positive points, Pam has her flaws—one of them is her temper. Like her mother, Pam has a hot and quick-to-ignite temper. When it comes to our girls, she can be like a momma bear defending her cubs. Pity the person who uses bad language in front of her girls or disrespects her in some way. Pam has a large well of patience and never loses her temper with the girls but she has a short fuse with me. I tend to be in her doghouse often. I admit that I usually deserve it.

We have two beautiful children. Natalie is eight and Gracie is four. Natalie is smart with strong opinions on everything. Gracie is the outspoken one. She repeats everything she hears and then adds her own twist to it. Her mother often will say something about what I have or haven't done and Gracie will call me on the carpet about it.

Gracie always carries a pink blanket she calls her Doot-Doot along with Mau-Mau, her white toy cat. None of us know what a Doot-Doot is or where she came up with the name. She couldn't say meow when she was little and it came out Mau-Mau.

I dressed in a blue tennis shirt, gray pants, and blue blazer. I looked in the mirror and felt good about what I saw. I was forty-three and still had all my black hair. I had lost weight in the past year since I started working out every day. At 6'2 and a 190 pounds, I was proud of myself.

I hustled downstairs to get the drinks ready. My father has to have a glass of Jack Daniels on the rocks as soon as he arrives. I know the first thing he will say, after hello, is "Eddie, where is my Jack?"

The doorbell rang. I could hear the kids yelling, "Grandmommy and Papa are here!" The kids scurry down the stairs and opened the door with Pam and me following.

I could hear activity at the front door with the kids and our dog Sunny, a black female lab, barking and Pam's two parrots talking loudly in the background. Sunny and the parrots often stayed with my parents when we are away and I think my parents love the pets more than they do me.

Pam is a pet person. I believe it's because she didn't have her own pet growing up. Pam told me she got Sunny for me but Sunny has been Pam's dog from day one. The dog follows her everywhere. Pam runs in the neighborhood and the dog runs with her. Sunny rides shotgun in the car whenever Pam does errands. The dog gets upset if someone rides in her seat.

When we first got married, Pam wanted a small bird. The small bird idea somehow evolved into a parrot that quickly escalated into two Amazon parrots. These parrots have a full repertoire of words and they mimic everything. In particular, they love to say "Girls!" in a loud scream. They learned this from Pam, who goes to the bottom of the stairs and yells up to the girls. The parrots often yell "Girls!" on their own and the kids will run downstairs thinking mom has called them.

Once my parents were inside and after the hellos are made, my father said, right on schedule, "Eddie, where is my Jack?"

My father is a handsome man. He is six feet tall, black hair with a touch of gray, and is in excellent shape. Everyone says I look like my father. I always like to hear that. My mother is a beautiful woman in her mid-sixties. She has smooth, wrinkle-free skin, brown eyes, blond hair, and a smile that lights up the room.

Teasing him, I said, "Dad, I'm sorry but I'm out of Jack Daniels. I do have some vodka."

He frowned and said, "Vodka? I would rather drink battery acid. Dear, don't take off your coat, we're leaving! This is supposed to be our anniversary party and he doesn't have my Jack!"

My mother pointed her finger at me and said, "Eddie, don't get him all worked up. You know how he gets."

I said, "Dad, you know I always have your Jack."

"Then why are you waiting? I should have it in my hand by now!"

We walked to the kitchen and I got the drinks. My mother, Pam, and the girls went upstairs to see the kids' newly redecorated rooms. Dad and I walked out to the deck.

My father asked, "Eddie, how's your practice doing?"

"Dad, it's going great! My billings are at an all-time high and my success rate is through the roof."

"That's great news!"

"How is business for you?"

He said, "It's good, like I've always told you—"

I interrupted him and said, "As long as people are still getting married there will always be a need for a good counselor to keep them together."

"I knew you would eventually learn something from me." He patted me on the shoulder.

I said, "A little has rubbed off."

"What are you doing different?"

"I changed my approach in determining whom I should counsel."

I explained my approach and the test. As I described it, he started to pace back and forth across the deck. When I finished he commanded, "I need another drink but make this one a double."

I went to the kitchen and refilled our drinks. My father uncharacteristically took the drink and gulped half of it quickly. He was standing an arm's length away from me. After a few seconds, he looked at me and in a harsh tone said, "You are an idiot!"

I was surprised. "What?"

"Your questionnaire is simply idiotic. It demeans the role of a woman in a marriage. The woman is simply being rated based on how she looks, how much she makes, if she can cook, and her choice of panties."

"Dad, I admit it's focused on the male, but that's my point. I'm helping the man recognize that he has a woman he should hold on to."

In a disgusted tone, he said, "Yes, because she wears the right panties!"

I tried to reason with him. "No, her choice of panties tells him if she's really interested in him. If a woman goes on a romantic weekend and doesn't wear something sexy, that's a problem! Also, a woman who wears sweatpants on a regular basis has given up."

My father said firmly, "No, maybe the granny panties and sweatpants are comfortable!"

Still trying to remain calm, I said, "My point is comfort shouldn't be her focus. On a romantic evening, she should be trying to appeal to her husband."

He finished his drink then said, "As I said before. You're an idiot! You have a doctorate from the University of Chicago and you boil a hundred years of social science down to 'does the woman wear flannel gowns or granny panties?'"

Starting to lose my patience, I said, "Dad, you're missing the point!"

In his fatherly tone, which I hate to hear, he said, "You should never, ever tell anyone what you told me. The licensing board will take your license away and you will be back to testing monkeys at the graduate school."

"You're overreacting. I'm only screening people to determine whom I can help. I want people's marriages to get better but I want to focus on those couples I can help."

Dad was upset and said, "Eddie, it's not about you! It's about the couple. Our job is to help people in their marriages."

"I can't rescue every puppy in the pound. Don't you always say that?"

"Yes, I do."

Trying to defuse the situation, I said, "When I interned with you, I remember you decided there were some couples you couldn't help."

"That's right, but only after I tried to help them, sometimes for years."

"I'm not like you. I want to invest my time with a couple I think I can help. If I focus on those and not everyone then it's better for me and for them."

I had made a good point. He walked to the deck rail and looked out over the backyard. He said, "Well, I agree with you on that."

He turned back to me and said, "Looking back, I should have ended it sooner with several couples. However, there are ones where it was tough but we made it. One couple in particular, I remember. The first summer you interned with me, do you remember the couple where the mother would come to the son's house to bathe him?"

"Oh yes, I think of that couple often. The man was forty when he married the woman who had been divorced twice before. The man had never been married and lived with his mother, who bathed him three times a week. The couple was having trouble because the man felt his wife wasn't treating him as well as his mother. The wife resented her husband's mother coming over to cook for him and bathe him."

"I wonder if your questionnaire would have allowed you to counsel them," he asked.

"Probably not."

He said, "That's what I thought. I continued to counsel them and they stayed together."

"How did you pull that off?" I asked.

"The man was actually a good husband but he had a few quirks. Over time, I convinced him it would be more fun if his wife bathed with him instead of his mom. I convinced his wife that having a good cook—his mother—come over from time to time wasn't such a bad thing. They're happy now."

"Dad, good for you! Now you're going to tell me the moral of the story right?"

"Yes I am. I never told them they should divorce. I stuck with them."

"I admire you for that. Now remember I don't tell the couples they should end the marriage. I simply tell them I won't counsel them and encourage them to find another counselor. I save them money and I save my energy. I believe each one of us has a limited amount of emotional energy we can give and I don't want to use it for people I can't help."

He added, "I believe you need to sometimes invest more of yourself with a couple than you do."

I clenched my fist. "I did. I struggled and I was depressed. Now I'm happy and I'm doing well. You should be happy for me!"

"It's hard to be happy for you when I think you're doing the wrong thing," he said in his fatherly tone.

"I'm not doing the wrong thing; I'm doing what works for me."

"How do you tell a couple after meeting them that you can't help them? I would find that hard to do."

"When I first meet a new couple, I tell them we will go through an evaluation period to see if we can work together. I tell them that I don't work with every couple."

"I don't think I could do that."

"I know. When I worked with you, there were couples I thought we couldn't help but you never turned down anyone."

He said, "I believe I have an obligation to help people."

"I do too, but not everyone."

Pam and my mother walked outside to the deck.

My mother said, "I can tell you two are talking about work. Now there will be no more discussion about work tonight! I don't want to hear about another couple's marriage and all those weird stories you both have. Some of the things you two talk about are creepy. I want to celebrate my marriage tonight."

My father said, "Dear, I agree, no more shop talk. Where are the girls?"

Pam said, "They're playing upstairs."

"I think I will go see them for a bit. Call me when we're ready to eat." My father walked inside.

My mother asked, "Are you two okay?"

"Yes, we were debating counseling techniques."

My mother said, "You know he's proud of you."

I replied, "He has an odd way of showing it."

"I know. He's old school."

The remainder of the evening went well and the dinner celebration was fun for everyone.

That evening before we went to bed, Pam asked, "Did you and your father have an argument tonight?"

"Yes."

"I thought so. He seemed upset. What was it about?"

I told her about his reaction to the screening test and that he thinks it's a bad idea to use it.

"Your mom is right. Your dad is old school. He has his way and you have yours."

"I had thought about writing an article about the screening test for publication in one of the professional journals and having him review it."

"I wouldn't. Publish it then tell him about it. If it's good, he'll be proud of you."

"I think you're right."

I went to bed thinking about my dad's reaction to the test. I should have listened to him. As usual, he was right.

CHAPTER 4

My wife is in the accounting business and her firm often has social events where prospective clients are invited. The day after my parent's anniversary dinner, her firm planned a dinner with several publishing companies and I went as usual. Pam likes me to attend because she says my stories about counseling couples are entertaining and I'm usually the hit of the party.

The dinner was in downtown Chicago at a fancy new age restaurant. We arrived at 6:00. An hour later, I had finished a couple of drinks and I was telling my stories. The evening was going well; people were laughing and asking questions about the couples I have counseled. When I returned from the washroom, a woman stopped me. She introduced herself as Susan Fairchild, an editor for a large publishing company.

Susan was in her early forties, attractive with short black hair and green eyes. She was wearing an expensive, well-fitted short black dress with a flashy diamond necklace.

Susan said, "Ed, I loved your stories."

"Well thank you! I hope you don't think I'm sharing too much about my couples."

"Not at all! I think your stories are gut-busting. The one where the wife had to dress up as a cartoon character and paint herself blue in order for the husband to be interested in her was hilarious."

"Believe me, it's a true story."

"And when the wife's mother walked in on them unexpectedly in their bedroom and her daughter was painted blue from head to toe. I couldn't stop laughing!"

"That was true too!"

"Have you considered writing a book?"

"No, I'm not a writer."

"Your stories would write themselves. I tell you what. Why don't you write down a few? We can meet when you have some time. I can read them and tell you if we can sell them. I bet we can."

"Seriously, you want me to write a book?"

"How do you think a book gets published? Someone has a good idea and writes a manuscript. An editor helps the person polish it, then boom! A book is born. Your stories could be a goldmine. Here's my card." She handed me a business card. "Once you have something, call me."

"Okay, I'll give it some thought. Thank you!"

"You're welcome! This is what I do; I find new stories to tell."

Susan walked back to the party. I stood there for a few minutes thinking about what she said. I was definitely interested.

The party finished late and from my observations, it was a success. Pam was in a good mood talking about the evening as we drove home. I decided to ask her opinion on writing a book.

"How well do you know Susan Fairchild?" I inquired.

"I know she's a rainmaker for her firm. Whatever book she publishes becomes a bestseller."

"Really?"

"Yes, she's the best. Why are you asking about her?"

"She asked me if I had ever considered writing a book on my counseling stories."

"No kidding! I have to agree, your stories are funny. I love the one about the college history professors who were married and always dressed up as Napoleon and Josephine. The woman dressed as Napoleon and the man dressed as Josephine. They started having trouble because he wanted to be Napoleon but she refused. You convinced them to pick a new couple from history. I still laugh when I think of the time I was at your office and they came out dressed as Cleopatra and Marc Antony. She was Marc Antony."

We laughed.

I said, "They spend a fortune on their costumes."

"I remember you telling me that."

"What do you think? Should I try to write a book?"

"Do you think you have the time to do it?"

"I don't know. Maybe I will write a few stories then see what you and Susan think about them."

"Oh no! Not me! I don't want to be involved. Do you remember when you asked me for comments on your speech? You didn't talk to me for a week."

"That was because you were too critical and tried to write it for me."

"Your speech read like one of your boring psych journals. I made your speech come alive. You can't handle critique."

"No, critique is fine but criticism is not."

She said, "See, we're arguing already. You publish the book, give me a signed copy, then I'll read it."

"That's fine with me. If you're okay with this, I think I'll give it a shot."

"I'm okay with it but remember we have our vacation planned. I don't want either of us working during the vacation or having to postpone it. I've worked for months to line this up."

"I agree."

"Also, you talked about using your dad for the article you wanted to write. My advice is the same for a book. I wouldn't get him involved."

"I agree."

My road to becoming an author started that night.

CHAPTER 5

I STARTED TO WRITE SOME of my stories but quickly discovered writing was difficult. I struggled with what I wanted to say and how to say it. I also found that when I tried to write I was easily distracted. I tried to write at home but there were always interruptions with the kids, with the pets, and from the home projects that I was supposed to do. Trying to write at work was also bad. I always had something to do there and I found myself working instead of writing. I tried writing at the library, coffee shops, and the park but I couldn't find the right place for me.

In order to get in my workout, I go to the gym early in the morning. My health club is in my office building. One morning after my workout, I had a cup of coffee, as I do every morning, at a trendy coffee shop in the atrium of my office building. I took my coffee and sat at a table to read the paper. The coffee shop was noisy so I went upstairs to the second floor of the health club where there is a basketball court. I sat on the bleachers and drank my coffee. No one is ever there in the morning so it was quiet. It would be perfect for me to go here early with my morning coffee and write. I was a basketball gym rat as a kid and the environment was comfortable for me.

I started to go there every morning to write. Soon the stories were flowing.

After a few weeks, I had written some stories and I decided to schedule a meeting with Susan to review them. I sent her an email with my stories attached. Her assistant quickly responded with an email setting up a meeting. I went to the meeting feeling good about what I had written.

Susan's office is in downtown Chicago in a modern office building on the top floor. Her assistant met me at the elevator. She was a pretty Hispanic woman in her late twenties with long, black wavy hair. She was wearing a white silk blouse, an expensive black pantsuit, and three-inch black pumps.

"Dr. Sterling, I'm Carla Rodriquez, I'm Ms. Fairchild's assistant." She spoke with a pleasant Spanish accent.

I said, "It's a pleasure to meet you."

"You too! Now this is your first meeting with Susan, correct?"

"Yes."

"Let me review the rules for meeting with her. One, ignore her if she yells. She hates the intercom and she forgets how to use it. Two, she might leave the office unexpectedly. You stay put; she will come back. Three, don't talk or ask about how she stores her files. She has a process that works for her. Four, there is no gum chewing. Five, you should never ask about her fiancé or any of her past engagements. Yes, she has had a few. The last rule is, don't ever accept any food she offers you. Do you have any questions?"

I swallowed hard and said, "I only met Ms. Fairchild once at a dinner party. I wonder if I'm meeting the right person."

"Was she drinking at the party?"

"Yes."

"You met the charming Susan. The other one is here today."

I was confused. Did she mean there was one Ms. Fairchild or two?

We arrived at Susan's office. According to Pam, Susan was a rainmaker for her company, which meant she had a large corner office. She had a commanding view of the Chicago skyline and Lake Michigan but the inside of the office was a mess. Files and manuscripts were stacked on chairs, on top of cabinets, tables, and the floor. Files were everywhere except on her desk. On top of her glass desk, situated in the corner, was a phone, an intercom, a tablet of paper, and a red pen, nothing else. No pictures or paintings were in the office. When I entered she was sitting at the desk with her back turned and was staring out the window.

"Ms. Fairchild, Dr. Sterling is here to see you."

Susan raised her hand with her index finger in the air as if she was saying to give her a minute.

Carla whispered, "She's meditating."

We stood there waiting for her. A couple of minutes passed. I was getting impatient but finally she turned in her chair. She stood and reached out her hand across the desk. Carla walked to the left of Susan and stood as if she was at attention.

"Dr. Sterling, it's good to see you again!"

I shook her hand. "It's good to see you too."

"Please have a seat. Would you like coffee and a donut? I make the donuts at home."

I looked at Carla; she smiled at me and gently shook her head no.

"I would like coffee but no thank you on the donut. I'm watching my weight."

Carla winked at me.

Susan asked, "Carla, could you bring us coffee?"

"Of course, how would you like your coffee?" Carla asked me.

"With cream please."

Carla left.

Susan said, "Now let's get down to it. I have a copy of your draft stories here." She walked to a tall pile of files teetering on a chair and pulled out a green folder. She walked back and sat at her desk. In a serious tone, she said, "I've read your stories. They're crap!"

Surprised, I said, "Really?"

"The stories aren't like the ones you told at the party. These are too clinical. You're not writing a speech for the marriage counselors' convention. People are going to pay real money for the book and the stories have to be interesting or funny. One boring story and the book is tossed. I have a book you should read that I think could help you."

She yelled, "Carla, please bring me a copy of Perkin's book."

Carla responded back on the intercom, "Okay."

Her harsh critique of my stories had shaken me and her shouting was unnerving. I wondered why she didn't push the button on the intercom. I have the same one in my office and it's simple to use.

She said, "Now I want you to tell this story to me the way you would tell it at a party." She points to a story of a couple from Indiana.

I took a second to gather my thoughts but before I could start, she got up and left the office without saying anything. A minute or so later Carla walked in with the coffee and a book.

I asked, "Where did Susan go?"

"I don't know, but don't worry, she'll come back. Here's your coffee and the book she asked for."

"Thanks! How long will she be gone?"

"You never know." Carla left.

I started drinking the coffee. I thumbed through the book then looked outside at the spectacular view.

Five minutes later, Susan came back and sat down. She stared at me and said, "I'm waiting for the story."

"Okay," I began. "The Parsons are from Munster, Indiana. The couple dated on and off for several years and finally got married. Mrs. Parson didn't notice anything unusual about him until they got back from their honeymoon. In a guest bedroom, which Mrs. Parson had not been in, Mr. Parson kept an expensive, anatomically correct, adult-size female doll. The doll was dressed in a silk teddy. This doll wasn't a cheap blow-up plastic doll but a doll with beautiful human hair, blue eyes, and realistic-looking skin. Somehow, he had the doll made to look like Mrs. Parson. She thought it was odd and tried hard to forget about it.

"A month after their honeymoon, they had an argument one night. She woke up the next morning and Mr. Parson wasn't in bed. She couldn't find him in the house so she checked the guest bedroom. Mr.

Parson was in the bed with the doll. Mrs. Parson freaked out and called me for an appointment. They came in and I counseled them.

"As it turned out, Mr. Parson was in love with the doll but he also loved his wife and didn't want to lose her. After weeks of discussion, I learned he had the doll made because he was convinced Mrs. Parson would never marry him so he wanted a doll that looked like her. When they did get married, he wanted his wife and the doll. I eventually convinced him his wife would be happier if the doll moved on. I first suggested he sell the doll or give it to someone but he was reluctant. I then learned there were male versions of the doll, so I suggested he buy a male doll and for the dolls to get married. He bought a doll that looked like him and had the dolls married in a ceremony in his backyard. I knew a museum curator and I asked him if he could use the dolls. He jumped at it. The doll couple moved to the museum and they are in a permanent display. Both couples are still happily married."

"Both couples! Now that's funny! See, when you say it the way you did, it's interesting and funny."

"I guess so."

"I want you to take these stories and rewrite them. Put in some of your humor. I want to see these next week."

"Next week?" I asked.

"You have a problem with that?" she asked in an imposing voice.

"Ah no, I can do it. Okay, I will see you next week."

"You have kids, don't you?"

"Yes."

Susan yelled, "Carla, pack a dozen of my donuts for Ed's kids."

Carla responded on the intercom, "Okay."

Susan said, "We're done, you can leave now."

Susan closed my file; she got up and put it back into the pile of folders.

As I left the office, Carla handed me a box of donuts. She whispered, "Remember what I told you and don't eat them!"

I said, "Okay."

Carla asked, "When does she want to see you again?"

"Next week and can we make it late in the week?" I asked.

"Does Friday at 3:00 work for you?"

"Yes, thank you."

On the drive home, I debated whether I wanted to continue with the book. I was convinced Susan was a loon—excuse me for using a diagnostic psychological term but she was a loon. I had always felt I could work with anybody but working with her was going to be difficult, I could tell already. Rewriting the stories would be hard to accomplish by when she wanted it but I thought I could get it done. After considerable debate, I decided to take one more step with the book.

As I arrived, Pam was just getting home from work. We met in the kitchen and I gave her a kiss.

She asked, "How was the meeting with Susan?"

"She's a loon."

"I've heard she is different. How did you determine so quickly she is a loon? Normally you psych guys need years and a ton of money to figure that out."

"It doesn't take a degree in clinical psychology to analyze her."

I put the donuts on the table and left the kitchen for the bathroom. As I returned, Pam was taking a bite from one. I remembered at that moment what Carla had said but it was too late. Pam's facial expression turned sour, she spit the donut out into a paper towel and said, "Oh my, that's awful!"

"Oh, I'm so sorry. Susan makes donuts and she brings them to the office. She wanted the kids to try them."

"It tastes like chocolate-covered sand!" She turned on the faucet and got a glass of water. She gulped it down.

I stood there as she recovered. I didn't tell her I had received a warning about the donuts. It would have only added to the situation.

"You said you've heard Susan is odd?" I pressed.

"Oh yeah! She's famous for her unusual behavior. However, she knows how to make a good book. She drives her authors crazy but they always produce for her. A few years ago, Susan left her job as an editor and became the managing partner. However, within a year, she moved back to senior editor. Apparently, a near mutiny occurred with the employees. She's not known as a people person."

"Now you knew this and you didn't tell me?"

"You wouldn't have believed me if I told you. I know how you are with people. You always want to make a clinical diagnosis on your own then you'll try to fix her."

"What do you mean 'fix her'?"

"You know how you're always analyzing people and then secretly try to change their behavior."

"I don't do that."

"Really? You're going to deny that?"

"Well maybe I do try to help people from time to time."

"Yeah right, 'from time to time.' You try to manipulate me all the time."

"No I don't. I don't manipulate. I guide people to make better decisions."

"I'm not going to get into an argument over that again. So other than learning she is a loon, what else happened?" asked Pam.

"She gave me good feedback and wants to meet again next week."

"Well that's good, but don't bring home any more of these." Pam dropped the box of donuts into the trash.

CHAPTER 6

I STARTED REWORKING THE STORIES and worked hard to finish them. I emailed Susan the revised stories late the evening before our meeting.

The next day, I was anxious on the way to the meeting. Susan's behavior last time had spooked me. As I parked in the garage below her building, my mouth and throat were dry, which often happens to me when I get nervous. In the lobby, there is a convenience store and I bought some gum. I opened two sticks and started to chew them.

At the elevator door, Carla met me and escorted me to Susan's office. Susan was sitting on the floor in what looked like a yoga position with her eyes closed. Carla and I stood there in silence until Susan opened her eyes, then Carla left. Susan seemed to be coming out of a trance, which took a few seconds. I stood there chewing gum and waiting.

She stared at me then pointed to my mouth and said, "Are you chewing gum?"

"Ah, yes, I am." I remembered the rule about the gum.

"Why are you chewing gum? I hate gum!"

"I'm sorry but my mouth was dry."

"If your mouth is dry, drink water!"

She started sniffing the air then wrinkled up her nose and said, "You're chewing spearmint! I hate the smell of spearmint!"

She yelled, "Carla! Bring the air freshener!"

She said to me, "Chewing gum is totally disrespectful. You are not a cow! Spit it out right now!"

She took a tissue from a box behind her desk and handed it to me. I took the gum out and placed it into the tissue. Carla walked in and sprayed the air with air freshener around the room then left. Susan went to her chair, sat down, and closed her eyes for a few seconds.

I stood there like a first grader holding the gum and waiting for my punishment. I slid the tissue with the gum into my pocket. After a few seconds, Susan opened her eyes and said, "I read the stories and they were excellent but I think we're missing something."

I sat down and was relieved the gum issue was behind us. I asked, "What are we missing?"

"The reader goes from one story to the next without a storyline behind them. We need to develop a story that ties everything together. Can you arrange the stories in chronological order?"

"Yes."

"On the white board, make two columns. Put the date of the story and story name in the first column. In the second column, list key events that were happening in your life or practice—getting married, having a child, a major success, winning the lottery, a major disappointment, whatever is significant to you."

She stood up and left the office. I was thinking about leaving as well. She totally freaked me out about the gum, which I then dug out of my pocket. I could smell the spearmint so I took more tissues and rolled it into a big ball then dropped it in the wastebasket.

I started to make the list she wanted. I wasn't quite done when she came back. She stopped at the door and sniffed the air as if she smelled the spearmint. She must have been satisfied because she walked over and stood next to me. She stood there for a few minutes reading.

She pointed to the board and asked, "What does this mean, *developed questionnaire*?"

"My practice was struggling then and I developed a questionnaire to help me select the couples to counsel."

"You mean a marriage counselor decides through a questionnaire whom he helps?"

"I do."

"Tell me all about the questionnaire and how you developed it."

She sat on the floor, crossed her legs, then motioned for me to sit down. I did. I told her about it. She laughed at the questions, the scoring system, and about the granny panties. When I finished she suddenly got up and left. I got up and sat in a chair.

A few minutes later, she came back. She said excitedly, "I can see the book's storyline now. The story is about how you were struggling in your practice until you developed the test. I will make you the hero of the marriage counseling profession because the test allowed you to help men to see the value in their relationships."

She yelled, "Carla, call Wilkins. I need him here in an hour. Tell him I know the Cubs are playing tonight but he needs to get here now!"

I asked, "Who is Wilkins?"

"Mike Wilkins will be your ghostwriter."

"Why do I need a ghostwriter?"

"I already have a book coming out next spring but the summer is a big reading time. I need a book for the summer and this will be it! The only way to get it done quickly is to add another writer. No one will ever know Mike helped you on this. We do this all the time with celebrities."

She started to pace back and forth then she stopped and said, "I have the book's name too: *Flannel Gowns and Granny Panties.*"

"What?"

"*Flannel Gowns and Granny Panties* will be the title and the subtitle will say, *The right panties can save your marriage!* The book cover will have an old fashioned flannel gown with a pair of cotton, pink granny panties hanging on a clothesline in front of a picket fence with a blue sky background."

I stared up at her and asked, "Are you sure that's a good title?"

Susan was excited and said, "Yes, it's perfect! It will be a bestseller. There will be a book tour with appearances on all the major TV entertainment and talk shows. This is big! We will make a fortune off this book!"

She walked out. I sat in the chair thinking about what she said. She was gone longer than usual. I started to wonder where she went and what she was doing. After ten minutes, she walked in with a man in tow.

"Ed, this is Lou Westlake, our managing partner. I told him about the book."

Lou said, "Dr. Sterling, it is a pleasure to meet you. I think your book idea is excellent. Susan always knows when a book is going to be a hit."

I didn't know what to say so I said, "Thank you!"

Lou said, "We are going to put this one on the fast track. Wilkins is our best ghostwriter. He will collaborate with you to get this done quickly. Susan has proposed a $50,000 advance. I hope it is acceptable?"

I was stunned at the price, but I knew I needed to play it cool. "Ah, I'll need to think about it."

"No problem, I will send you our standard contract on Monday. Please have your attorney look it over, sign it, and we can get started."

Susan stood there smiling. I had come to her office with a few stories and I was about to sign a book contract. I was overwhelmed.

Lou said, "I would like to suggest we go across the street to our favorite bar and have a drink to celebrate. Our staff goes there on Friday and we always have a good time. Can you go for a while?"

"Sure," I said.

Lou said, "Let's go."

Susan said, "I'll meet you there."

Lou and I walked across the street. Soon the bar was crowded with people from the publishing company. Lou introduced me to dozens of people. The news must have spread like wildfire because everyone from the firm seemed to know about the book.

Susan walked up with a man and introduced me to Mike Wilkins. He was wearing a Cubs jacket and hat. He seemed to be a nice fellow and asked if we could meet the next morning. Pam was out of town with the kids for the weekend so the timing was perfect. He left after having a drink to go to the Cubs game.

Susan drank as we talked and a transformation started to occur. The fast-talking, pushy woman with several personality quirks became dramatically different. She was calm and charming.

I had three martinis in less than two hours with no food and I was starting to get a good buzz. I knew I needed to get out of there before I did or said something to ruin my book deal. In addition, I needed to be back downtown the next morning at 9:00. I said goodbye to everyone and started to leave.

At the front door, Susan cornered me and asked, "Did your family like my donuts?"

I was thinking I should be kind so I lied and said, "Oh they loved them!"

"Oh that's great; I took the liberty of bringing some of my cookies. They're a new recipe." She took a box from inside her bag and gave it to me.

"I'll see you in the morning!" She walked away.

I walked outside and the fresh air hit me. I was a little dizzy so I decided to leave my car in the garage and take a cab home. On the way home, I was starving and had to fight the urge to have a cookie. Remembering how bad the donuts were, I decided to leave the cookies in the cab.

CHAPTER 7

I SET THE ALARM FOR 7:00 and I had a hard time getting up. I'm not much of a drinker and three martinis was a lot for me. I wasn't hungover but I did have a headache. I took two aspirins, showered, dressed, called a cab, and had a quick breakfast. I arrived at Susan's office at 9:00. Carla met me at the elevator. She was dressed as if it was a normal workday, again in a beautiful suit. We walked through the empty office.

I asked, "So do you often work on Saturdays?"

"Yes, my schedule is unpredictable. Susan often calls me late, like she did last night, and I have to be here."

"Sounds like you put in a ton of hours."

"Yes I do but the pay is excellent."

"How long have you worked with Susan?"

"Five years," she said. Pride was evident in her voice. "Susan went through nine assistants before me."

"Wow, nine. You must get along well with her."

"Yes, we're a team. She loves me and takes care of me. I do the same for her."

"Is she hard to work for?"

"Now that I know there are two Susans it's easier. Before then, it was tough."

"How do I keep her from giving me food?"

She laughed then said, "I told you not to take any. Now you have to take whatever she gives you or she will be offended. You should know she's making cookies now."

"I know, she gave me some last night."

"Did you try them?"

"No, I was afraid to. Are they as bad as the donuts?"

"They're worse. Our mailroom guy publishes a rating on what she makes. He keeps the rating on the network and we all check it. He gave the cookies two thumbs down; the donuts were one thumb down."

"The cookies are worse, that's good to know." I thought of the cab driver; I hoped he didn't try any.

I asked, "If the rating's on the network, can't Susan see it?"

"No, she doesn't know how to turn on a computer. She hates technology. Her cell phone is an early flip phone. The only reason she uses it is because she can't find payphones."

She led me to Susan's office. Carla said, "Susan, Ed is here to see you."

Susan was sitting in her chair with her back turned. As she did before, she raised her hand with her index finger in the air as if she was saying to give her a minute. Mike Wilkins was sitting in a chair. I sat in a chair next to him. Carla left. After a minute or so, Susan turned around and said, "Mike you know the drill, run with it."

She turned back around and looked out the window. Mike took control and started to ask questions about my practice, my family, and me. Two hours passed with Mike asking questions. Susan never asked a question or turned around.

At 11:00, she turned around in her chair and said, "Okay, we have enough. We'll have the first draft in two weeks. We'll send it to you. You should plan to be here for a day to review it. Ed, you can leave."

As I left, Susan yelled, "Carla, give Ed cookies for his kids."

I stopped and Carla handed me a bag.

Carla said, "Wait a second and I'll walk out with you." She put on her coat and walked with me.

I asked, "Are you done for the day?"

"Yes. Susan and Mike will stay. Once she starts one of these, she and Mike will work late, start early tomorrow and do it every day until a draft is ready for review. I have to order them food because she won't let him leave to eat. She'll push him hard."

"It sounds like it's going to be a tough period coming for him."

"Yes it is. They'll hate each other when the book is finished. He'll work with her until the book is completed then he'll quit for a few months. They won't talk at all during the recovery period then she'll need him again. They will then get back together for the next book."

I stepped into the elevator but she stayed back, holding the elevator door open with her hand. I asked, "Why do they keep working together?"

"She's the best editor in the business and he's the best ghostwriter. They need each other. After each book, I say to myself they aren't going to work together again but they always do. The process will be hard on you too. Once a draft is ready, your role will start and you will find it difficult as well. Now before I forget, here's a card for a photographer we use. Susan wants you to take your best blue suit, a red tie, and a white button-down suit to the studio. Please call and make an appointment. We need you to do this by next Wednesday." She gave me a card.

The elevator reached the bottom floor. I got my car and drove home. I was hungry and I sampled a cookie on the ride home. The mailroom guy was right—the cookies were two thumbs down. I tossed them into the trash when I got home.

CHAPTER 8

ON MONDAY, I RECEIVED A draft contract. I sent it to my attorney and he recommended a few changes. He called Susan's attorney and quickly they agreed on the contract language. By 5:00 PM on Tuesday, I had signed a book deal. Three days later, a check arrived for $50,000. Pam got home from her trip the day the check arrived and she was ecstatic about the book deal. I hadn't told her about the contract because the entire situation still seemed unreal to me. The check made it real. Pam took pictures of me posed with the check.

Pam looked at the check and in the check's memo section it read, *Advance for Flannel Gowns and Granny Panties.*

She inquired, "Is this a mistake?" She pointed to the memo line.

"No that's the book's title."

"I thought the book was about your counseling stories."

"It is."

She asked skeptically, "So how does that title make sense for a counseling book?"

"Susan thought it would be a catchy title."

"So do you discuss lingerie with your clients?"

"I know it sounds strange but lingerie is often discussed in counseling sessions."

Surprised, she asked, "You're kidding?"

"No, panties are discussed in depth in a couple of my stories. I can tell you some details if you'd like."

Pam held up her hand. "No, I don't want to know. I said I would read the published book. Now please promise me you aren't writing a porn novel."

"I promise."

We all went out to dinner and celebrated the book deal.

The following week, I went to the photographer. I was expecting a simple headshot but it was a full photo shoot with a makeup person and a hair stylist. The stylist cut, washed, and styled my hair. The makeup woman brushed away my worry lines and blemishes. The photographer took what seemed like a thousand pictures, but I have to say I looked good in the pictures.

I went to work as usual for the next two weeks. Then on a Wednesday morning at the office, I got a special delivery that contained the first draft of the book with a handwritten note from Susan. She asked me to read the draft and be prepared to discuss it on Saturday morning at 9:00.

Also included in the package was the book cover, which was exactly as Susan described. The cover, with the flannel gown and pink panties on a clothesline against the blue sky, was indeed eye-catching. The picture of me on the back cover, in my humble opinion, was outstanding. I showed the book cover to my assistant, Sally, and she said she would buy the book simply because of the cover.

I read the draft and was amazed at how exciting my professional life seemed. The story of how I helped people in their marriages was heroic and that made me a little uncomfortable. I found some factual errors and I made some minor edits but overall I was impressed. I was ready for the Saturday meeting—or at least I thought I was.

On Saturday at 9:00 sharp, I arrived at Susan's office and Carla met me at the elevator. After greetings, we walked to Susan's office.

She cautioned me, "Today will be difficult and you will have to have patience. You will see the editing process with Susan can be chaotic."

"What do you mean by chaotic?"

"Susan can get emotional at times during editing. You will have to stand your ground if you feel strongly about something or she will run over you."

"Thanks for the advice."

"Other authors have left her office crying before. So please keep your emotions in check."

"I will try. Do all the editors work like Susan?"

"No, she's unique."

As we get near the office, I could hear Susan and Mike yelling. Carla stopped at the door and said in a quiet voice, "Remember to stay calm."

When I entered the office, Susan and Mike were standing a few feet apart and were visibly upset.

Mike yelled, "Let me dumb this down for you so you can understand. The Cubs have to get better pitching!"

Susan yelled back, "You're telling me *you* have to dumb something down for *me*? I always use third grade words to tell you anything and you know as much about baseball as you do about writing. The Cubs have the arms to win but they don't have the bats to produce the runs."

Mike screamed, "You never look at the stats. You go with your emotions! They need pitching, and by the way, I'm the best writer you have."

I interrupted and said, "Good morning! I love the Cubs and I have an opinion on their pitching—"

"Stay out of this!" Susan screeched.

I sulked to a chair and sat down. For the next few minutes, they argued about the Cubs. Their argument got hotter and they started cursing at each other. I didn't know whether I should leave or call for the riot squad. All of sudden Susan walked out. Mike walked over and sat down in a chair next to me. He took out his phone and looked at it. He didn't seem the least concerned about the shouting match with Susan.

A minute passed and I said, "I liked the draft."

"Thanks," he said coolly.

"So do you want to hear my comments?"

"No, we should wait, Susan needs to hear them."

"Is she upset about your argument?"

"What argument?"

"Weren't you two arguing a couple of minutes ago?" I asked, wondering how he couldn't remember the shouting match that just occurred.

"No, we were talking about the Cubs."

"You normally curse at people when you discuss the Cubs?"

In a hostile tone, he quipped, "Are you a choir boy or something?"

I was surprised and said, "That's an aggressive response. Let me ask you something. You have never been married, am I right?"

"Yes, how did you know?"

"Women tend to shy away from men who have anger issues."

He replied quickly, "I don't have anger issues! I have strong opinions."

"About everything, right?"

"Well, most things," he said slowly.

"No, I can tell you have strong opinions on all things."

"Well maybe."

"I bet your friends often comment about your temper."

Mike looked away and said quietly, "Yes."

"You are never physical with anyone but you are often loud and aggressive."

"Yes."

"Have you ever had a girlfriend break up with you because of your temper?"

"Well...."

"Just say yes."

"Yes."

I asked, "I bet you follow politics closely?"

"Yes, I do."

"Are you a Democrat?"

"Yes."

"You have no pets, right?"

"Correct."

"You don't like change but you love technology, right?"

"Right again."

"You love computer games, right?"

"Yes. How do you know these things?"

"I listen and I observe."

Mike said, "You seem know me well. Maybe I should come to see you sometime to talk."

"I would like that."

Susan walked in then sat down in her chair. She asked, "Ed, how did you like the draft?"

"I liked it but I have a few edits and some comments."

"Fine, let's hear them."

Susan turned her chair and looked out the window. I started to review the draft page by page. Mike listened, asked questions, and took notes. It took two hours to complete my review.

Once I finished, Susan turned, looked at me and said, "The errors we will change and I like some of your edits but I will not change the storyline to make you look less heroic. People want to read about heroes. You change people's lives and you save marriages because your counseling process works. You make men recognize the women they have are worth keeping then you help the men and women to change. That is the storyline. If you don't like it, then leave!"

My eyebrows rose up on my forehead. "I'm no hero. I'm not a firefighter or police officer. I talk to people and sometimes I can help them change."

She slammed her hand down on the desk and said, "Look at the people in these stories! They are broken people whom you rescued!"

"No, I don't do that."

"Yes, you do! For example, the funeral director story, his family was in the funeral business for four generations. He grew up and played around dead people. He could only sleep with his wife if the room was cold. That guy was broken and you fixed him."

"No, I didn't fix him. As a child, he saw terrible things that he kept bottled up. He had never opened up with anyone about his life. I helped him open up to me and to his wife. I helped him see that being with a warm, caring woman was much better than being than being with a cold, dead one."

Susan asked, “Is the couple still together?”

“Yes, they are happy and they have a child now.”

“See, you fix people!”

“My counseling is just what any good counselor does. What I did that is different was develop a test to determine which couples I should help.”

“No, it is more than that. You have a counseling style and personal manner that allows people to open up and connect with you. Throughout your stories, you have your tips for having a good marriage. For example, in one story you said a man should always talk to his wife as if he was first dating her. When people first start to date, you said they listen better.”

“It’s true and I always stress the importance of listening with my couples.”

“You also said a couple should treat their marriage as if it is a long date.”

“I tell that to every couple and I also practice it in my marriage.”

Susan said, “Another piece of wisdom you stated was a person in a relationship must define what the boundaries are. A person must say what he or she is willing to do and won’t do. You described that in the story of the man’s mother who moved in and took over the family. She took over the cooking, cleaning, taking care of the kids, and paying the bills. The wife’s role became solely bringing home a paycheck. You worked with the man to help him understand his wife needed to set boundaries and it was okay for her to establish them.”

“That is also one of my rules to a happy marriage.”

“I have an idea. We need to write down your marriage rules. What if we developed Dr. Sterling’s Seven Marriage Rules? Each story will use one or more of your seven rules.”

Mike asked, “Why not ten? Like the ten commandments?”

“No, the ten commandments or ten golden rules have been used in other books. Seven is also my lucky number.”

I said, “Geez, I don’t know if I have seven.”

Susan said, “You just mentioned three and we can quickly develop four more. It has to be seven. Let’s work on them now.”

I said, "I need to call home if we are going late."

Susan replied sarcastically, "I bet you have to ask mommy's permission to stay out late."

"No, I'm practicing what I preach to my couples. You should communicate changes in plans as soon as you know them."

Susan smiled and said, "See, there's another one that we can use."

I asked, "How long will we be here today?

"We will stay until we have the seven rules done," Susan said firmly.

"Geez, okay, let me make a quick call home."

I was annoyed at Susan regarding her comment so I stepped outside and called Pam's cell. I knew Pam would be at the soccer field. She answered on the second ring.

I said, "This is going to take longer than I expected. I won't be able to get to the girls' soccer practices today."

"Sounds like you're going to have to work for the $50,000."

"Seems like it."

"No problem, the girls are with me. I can take care of it. Besides, you always whine when you have to go to the girls' practices."

"I don't whine, I simply make my feelings clear to you."

She said, "There you go using your counselor speak on me again. I know whining when I hear it."

"Anyway, thanks!"

"Okay, love you!" she said.

"Love you too!" I hung up and I was hurt a bit about the whining comment.

I went back into Susan's office and she had already listed two more rules. The remainder of the day we argued on what the seven rules were. Susan would come up with a catchy rule then she would get upset if I rejected it. I wouldn't use one unless I had used it in my practice. By late afternoon, we had come up with the seven rules. Susan wanted more stories and I would have to tie the rules to the stories. She wanted a draft of the new stories in two weeks.

The book was fast becoming a second job.

CHAPTER 9

Pam manages her time well but me not so much. Sally keeps me on schedule at work and Pam keeps me on schedule at home. Pam and Sally give me lists of things I need to do and when I need to do them. I'm supposed to merge the lists to manage my day. I don't always do that and things fall in the cracks. Pam says I'm absent-minded but I don't think so. I think I focus on what are the most important things. I make Pam angry often about the things I forget or because I run late, which upsets her carefully engineered schedule.

Pam has a ritual she does when she is really mad at me. She will turn off the garage door opener, lock the back door, then I have to go to the front door and ring the bell to get in. Don't ask why I have to follow this ritual but that's the rule. I think her mother used it with her dad.

I had been working hard since the last meeting with Mike and Susan. I was tired and I was starting to forget things. After a particularly hard day, I arrived home to find the garage door wouldn't open. I sat in the car cursing. I went through in my mind what I was supposed to have done for Pam or the girls but I couldn't think of anything. I checked my pockets and my briefcase for Pam's to-do list then I remembered I left it on my desk. I grabbed my briefcase and walked dejectedly to the front door. I looked around to make sure the neighbors weren't watching. They all know when I go to the front door and ring the bell that I'm in trouble. Unfortunately, Ricky who lives across the street was outside and saw me. He loves it when Pam locks me out.

He yelled, “Are you in trouble again?”

I waved without looking at him.

Ricky yelled, “Do you need a marriage counselor? I hear your dad is a good one.” He always yelled the same thing. I wanted to give him the finger but I only waved.

I rang the bell. I heard someone struggling with the door and finally Gracie opened it. She was standing there with her Doot-Doot in her left hand holding it up to her face and Mau-Mau under her arm.

I asked, “Hi monkey, can you let me in?”

Gracie wrinkled her face and said, “We mad!”

“We are? I mean, who is mad at me?”

“Mommy mad, sister’s mad and me mad.”

“You mean ‘I am mad too.’”

Gracie had a puzzled look and asked, “Daddy, you mad?”

“No sweetie, I meant…never mind. Why is Mommy mad?”

“You missed Natalie’s recital.”

I smacked by head with my hand and exclaimed, “Oh no! Was it today?”

Gracie said, “Yes, we mad!”

“Can you let me in and let me apologize?” I begged.

Gracie said firmly, “I have to talk to Mommy.”

She closed the door. I stood there embarrassed.

Ricky yelled over, “Do you want me to call your dad? He will probably give you a family discount.”

I don’t look back but this time I give him the finger.

Ricky laughed then yelled, “I hear he is good at anger management too!”

The front door opened again.

Gracie said, “Mommy says you can come in.”

“Thank you sweetie!”

Gracie unlocked the storm door and I walked in. I leaned over to kiss her but she ran to the front room. Pam was sitting there on a chair like a judge. The girls were on the couch, waiting for me like a jury. They all had a serious look. I know I'm in deep trouble. Even the dog looked mad at me. She was sitting on the floor next to Pam. Normally Sunny would have met me at the door but not today.

I looked at Pam and said in my most humble voice, "Pam, I'm so sorry."

Pam held up her hand and said defiantly, "You talk to Natalie first!"

I turned to Natalie and said, "Nattie, I'm so sorry for missing your recital."

"That's okay, Daddy," she said with tears in her eyes.

"How did it go?"

Pam said, "She didn't miss a note. I was so proud. I took a video of it."

"Thank you for doing that. Girls, I'm so sorry. That was terrible for me to forget the recital. Please forgive me!" I pleaded.

Natalie said, "Daddy, I forgive you!" She stood and I kissed her.

Gracie looked at her mom and asked, "Do I forgive Daddy?"

Pam smiled and said, "Yes Gracie, you do."

Gracie said, "I forgive you too." She stood and hugged me. I kissed her.

I turned to Pam and asked, "Do you forgive me?"

"Not yet. Where is my to-do list?" she demanded.

"At the office."

She grilled me, "How often are you supposed to check the list?"

"Three times a day."

"Did you?"

"No. I'm sorry. I promise I will do a better job with that. Do you forgive me now?"

She smiled and said, "Only if you buy us dinner."

For a second, I thought I need to work on the book but my better judgment prevailed and I said, "Of course, what do we want to eat?"

Natalie yelled, "Pizza!"

Gracie yelled what she always said: "Nuggets!"

I said, "Great, we are having nugget pizza!"

I stepped over and put my arms around Pam then kissed her.

I said, "I'm sorry."

"I know. Now let's go, I'm starved."

Sunny now nuzzled up against me, looking for affection. I bent down to her and said, "You're supposed to love me regardless. You are a traitor!" I patted her head.

Pam said, "She's female. She knows when we're mad at you."

I laughed. We walked to the car and on the way out Ricky yelled, "So she took you back!"

I waved and I wanted to give him the finger again but my family was there.

Over dinner, I watched the video. Natalie had done a great job and I was sad I missed it. Pam told me that since I had started working on the book I had been distracted. I agreed with her but didn't know what to do about it.

When we arrived home, I went across the street to visit Ricky. He was on the back deck. Ricky, a lieutenant colonel in the Marine Corp Reserves with three tours in the Gulf, is married to Pam's cousin and her best friend, Brenda. He was a fighter pilot and he approaches life like one, always ready to charge ahead. He is 6'2 and 200 pounds of all muscle. His black hair is short and he has a lean, square face. He looks like the guy on the Marine recruiting poster. He is also a commercial airline pilot.

His wife, Brenda, is a pretty blonde who takes no crap from him, which is why they get along so well. She is a perfect example of a woman who established clear boundaries for her husband. My girls are scared of Ricky because he talks in a loud, Marine-like voice. They think he is always yelling at them. Pam ignores his loud Marine demeanor and stands up to him like Brenda does.

As I stepped onto the deck, he turned to me with a beer in his hand and said sarcastically, "There he is—your name is Ed, isn't it? It's been so long I'd almost forgotten you."

"Give me a break! I've been busy lately."

"Yeah, Pam told Brenda you've been working on a book. She told me the title—let me think for a second, I believe it was something like 'let me help you end your marriage.' Am I close?"

"No, you're nowhere close! Did you forget to get your dementia prescription filled again?"

"No, I got it the same day you asked me to pick up your erectile dysfunction prescription, remember?"

"You're so funny! Do you pilots spend your time in the cockpit practicing to become comedians?"

"Yes we do. I've been thinking about becoming a standup when I retire."

"I wish you luck with that. I wanted to ask you a favor."

"Sure, what do you need?"

"I'll have a draft ready soon and I know you read on your trips. Could you read it and comment on it?"

"Sure, I would be happy to. Will reading it improve my marriage?"

"You do what Brenda tells you to do and you will be fine."

"I've been doing that for twenty years."

I said, "Also, please don't talk to anyone about the book other than Brenda. The publisher doesn't want the book name or topic to be known."

"No problem, I'm a Marine. We know how to keep secrets."

I stayed for a while and had a beer. It felt good to relax. I finished the work on the book late the next evening and sent it via email to Susan.

CHAPTER 10

I WAS LOOKING FORWARD TO going on vacation. There would be no work—and in particular, there would be no Susan to worry about. She was starting to wear on me. I had told Susan a dozen times we were going on vacation and she never said a word, then two weeks before we were to leave, she asked me to postpone it. I told her I couldn't postpone and she got upset. She said none of her other authors would ever consider leaving town in the middle of a book.

We were going to Disney World. This was the first time we had been there and the trip was going to be a big event. We were spending five days at the park, another couple of days in other parks, then five days at the beach.

We flew from Chicago to Orlando on a Saturday. On Sunday, we went to Magic Kingdom and the kids had a blast. They saw every Disney character and had lunch with a princess. Gracie insisted on getting every princess dress that Disney had. I never knew Disney had so many princesses.

On Monday, we went to Epcot. That afternoon I started getting text messages from Susan—she wanted to talk. I texted back I could not. She insisted. I ignored the texts. She started to call every hour then every fifteen minutes. I turned off my phone. I didn't want to talk to her. That evening she called the hotel and Pam answered. Pam didn't know Susan had been hounding me all day. She handed me the phone and gave me her serious look, which I read as *You aren't supposed to be working.*

I said, "Hello."

Susan said, "Why have you not called me? I've been trying to get in touch with you all day."

I said in a loud voice so Pam could hear, "Susan, I'm trying to spend time with my family."

Susan replied in an angry tone, "Hey I'm not deaf; you don't have to yell at me!"

I lowered my voice and said, "I saw you on Friday and everything was fine. What's wrong?"

"We did a book group review this morning. Everyone feels we need another story but it needs to be a sad story. One where you tried your best but the couple still divorced because the issues were insurmountable. It would be good if the guy was a real jerk or weird in some way."

I turned my back so Pam wouldn't hear me and I asked, "Okay, when do you need it?"

"Tomorrow."

"I can't do it by tomorrow. We have big plans tomorrow."

"Tomorrow night."

"Susan, I will be at the beach in a few days. I'll write one up then."

"What if I flew down tomorrow and we ducked out? We could knock it out fast. It would take only a few hours."

"Susan, no! I can't get away."

"I know Pam is the boss of your family. Let me talk to her and I'll explain to her our problem."

"No, I'm not going to do that! Pam's not my boss!"

Susan chuckled then replied, "Yeah, you should keep telling yourself that. You call her when you need to go to the bathroom."

"Susan, I'm not going to discuss my marriage with you." I rushed on before she could interrupt. "I have to think of a story and then I need some time to write it. Over the next couple of days, I'll think of one, I'll write it up when we get to the beach. I'll have some downtime then."

"When exactly is that?"

"I'll be at the beach on Friday."

"I expect an email on Saturday morning."

"I'll try."

She hung up.

Pam said immediately, "You're not working on the book, this is our vacation!"

"I agree, I told Susan the same thing. We'll have some downtime when we get to the beach; I can work on what she wants then."

"Yeah, that's okay. I'll have to make a couple of calls back to the office by then too."

I was pissed Susan had called. She has no life outside the office and I wasn't surprised she wanted me to use my vacation time. I still don't know how she found our hotel. No one knew except for Sally and Rebecca and they didn't tell her.

Over the next couple of days, I thought of several couples with sad stories but I kept coming back to a couple I counseled in the third year of my practice. One afternoon a man showed up at my office without an appointment. Sally had stepped out to do a quick errand so the door to my reception area was open. I heard someone enter the office so I got up to see who it was.

I was startled when I saw the man. He was short, around four and a half feet or so, and heavy for his height with no discernable neck. He was bald on top and the brown hair around his ears stuck out like a clown. I know it's not nice to say but he was an ugly man. His clothes were simple: a black T-shirt, jeans, and running shoes. I first thought he was probably a challenged individual who might have gone to the wrong office.

I asked, "May I help you?"

He didn't look directly at me; he looked a little off to the side. He asked in a quiet voice, "Are you Dr. Sterling?"

"Yes, I am."

"I would like to talk to you about counseling my wife and me."

I said, "Normally, you would need an appointment but I have an opening now. Please come in."

We went into my office.

I said, "Have a seat."

"Do you mind if I stand?"

"No, do you mind if I sit?"

"No."

I sat down. He started to pace back and forth in front of my desk.

I asked, "May I have your name?"

"Yes, I'm Raymond Devon."

I thought for a second. "Are you Raymond Devon of Devon Investments?"

"Yes."

"It's a pleasure to meet you. Your business is the largest commodities company in the nation. I saw a TV show about Devon Investments and how you pioneered using computers to trade commodities."

"Yes, I'm a complete nerd."

"Very successful from what I hear. How may I help you?"

"My wife and I are having some trouble. I would like for us to come and see you."

"Is your wife willing to come?"

"Yes."

"That's good; please tell me about you two."

For the next thirty minutes, he told me his story. His father was a commodities trader and he taught Raymond about them. Raymond started using computers to improve their trades and the business boomed. He inherited the business when his father died. Raymond's first marriage ended after two years and she left with a fortune. Losing the money didn't worry him because he made money easily but losing her hurt him deeply. He thought she loved him but learned that she only loved him for his money. Now, he felt his current marriage of nearly three years was in trouble. He showed me pictures of his ex-wife and his current wife. They were stunningly beautiful. I found out later they were models. He said he loved his wife terribly and would do anything to keep her. He wanted desperately for her to love him.

In tears, he described how people perceived him. He described himself as an ugly troll. From childhood, people told him he was ugly. He felt his intelligence and his ability to use computers saved him. I found him to be a brilliant, kind but troubled man and I wanted to help him. I told him I would like to talk to his wife. She called the next day and scheduled an appointment.

When Mrs. Devon came in, her pictures didn't do her justice. She was even more stunning in person. She was tall, with a model's figure, long black hair and dark blue eyes. She was dressed in designer clothes, designer shoes and was carrying a designer purse. She made it clear in the first few minutes she was unhappy and she was thinking about a divorce. I asked her if she was willing to do counseling with Raymond and she was. I learned later that she only went to counseling because it was required in her prenuptial agreement with Raymond.

I learned she mistreated and bullied Raymond. She wouldn't take a picture with him or be in public with him. When they vacationed, it was always out of the country in some remote spot. They had separate bedrooms even on vacations and when they did get together, the room had to be dark.

Over a period, she opened up to me and I learned she regretted marrying Ray but she loved the lifestyle his money provided. The only reason she was still with him was that their prenup had a three-year wait period. I knew they would never stay together. No amount of counseling would ever change her heart.

I thought Raymond had gotten a raw deal in his marriages but he did have to take partial ownership. He had married the wrong type of woman. His wives were socialites who wanted the glitter, the nice lifestyle and being around pretty people that money brings. Raymond wasn't an attractive person but he was kind, gentle, and loving.

I eventually helped him though the divorce and I continued to counsel him. Over time, I helped him realize he needed to accept the fact that his vision of a wife would be hard to hold onto. He thought his money caused him to look better to women. I helped him realize if the woman doesn't have a good heart that his money would only change her perception of him for a while. I helped him to start dating again. Eventually he found a woman who accepted him as he was. She was a plain woman. She had a great heart and loved Raymond unconditionally. They have been married four years and they are happy.

Once we got to the beach, I wrote up the story and sent it to Susan. She loved it and included it.

Later when the book came out, I got a card from Raymond. He told me how much I had helped him and thanked me again for making his new life so happy. I cried when I read the card.

CHAPTER 11

WHEN I GOT BACK FROM vacation, I met with Mike and Susan often. Susan's odd behavior, which was barely tolerable before, got worse. Her habit of getting up and leaving our meetings increased and so did her yelling. She and Mike argued over minor wording constantly. I hated to be with them. I started to phone in to the meetings because their behavior was so bad.

One afternoon, I got a call from Carla.

"Ed, this is Carla. I wanted to tell you Susan will be out of the office for a while."

"Is she okay?"

"She needed to get away for a bit."

"Sounds like she may be ill or something?"

"Don't worry, she'll be back soon. I'll call you with a date when you can meet with her."

"Do you have a feel for how long she'll be out?" I asked.

"Probably three to four weeks. She needed to get away for a bit."

"You sure she's okay?"

"Yes. Mike is working on the book and will send you another draft soon. Once you get it, please review and send back your comments."

"I will."

She hung up. My gut told me there must be something wrong with Susan because Carla said the same thing twice to me. I decided not to ask anything else about it and simply wait for the next draft.

Two weeks later on a Friday evening, I got a package. In it was a draft of the book and a note from Carla. The note said I was to proofread the draft and call Mike with any changes. I read the draft over the weekend and it was great. I made a few edits but the book was coming together well. I called Mike on Monday with my suggestions and the conversation went well. He was receptive to all of them. He said he would give me a draft in a week.

The next Monday, I received the draft with a note from Carla. Susan wanted to meet with Mike and me on Saturday. She asked me to make sure I had read the new draft and come prepared to discuss the book.

On Saturday, I was ready for the meeting and arrived at 9:00. Carla met me at the elevator.

"Good morning, Ed."

"Good morning to you. How is Susan?"

"She's back in the saddle and charging hard."

"That's a good thing, right?"

"Yes, it is. Now next Saturday evening, we are having a holiday party at 6:00. Please be there if possible. It will be a big event. Several bookstore executives will be there and we plan to introduce you to them as the first marketing step for the book. Please bring your wife. Here is the invitation."

She handed me an envelope.

"I'll be there."

"The meeting will be different for you today."

"What do you mean?"

"You'll see."

Carla walked me in. Susan and Mike were there already. From the beginning, the atmosphere was different. Susan was calm, there was no yelling, and she never left the room. She used the intercom to Carla twice. She seemed to be a different person.

Mike drove the review. Several times, Mike asked Susan's opinion on wording and she said either his wording was fine or she asked my opinion. This behavior I hadn't seen before. In the past, all decisions on wording were hers. By noon, we were done. Mike and I left together.

On the elevator, I said, "That went well. You're doing a great job!"

"Yes it did and thanks for the compliment! I was prepared to do battle with her but it didn't happen. I can tell she isn't feeling well."

"Has she been sick?"

Mike immediately clammed up and ignored my question. He said, "This is going to be a great book! I think people will love it. Your stories are interesting and funny."

I wondered why he avoided the subject but I let it pass. I said, "Thanks! You've pulled together the stories along with the Sterling Rules into a fun-to-read book."

"I have to give the credit to Susan. She knows how to knit these things together. I'll have a new draft ready soon. It's time to have some people critique it."

"I have a couple of my friends lined up to read it."

The elevator opened and he said, "That's good, have a good weekend!"

"You too."

I walked away feeling as if we had passed a major milestone with the book. I was looking forward to some downtime and the holiday party.

CHAPTER 12

THE NEXT SATURDAY, PAM AND I planned to go to the holiday party but the girls were sick. Rebecca was out of town so Pam decided to stay at home. Susan was waiting for me when I arrived. I was trying to judge which Susan was there. I hoped it was the nice Susan and it was.

She took me around and introduced me to several bookstore executives. All of them were aware of the book and Susan had me tell some of my stories. The executives enjoyed them and said they were looking forward to the release date. One of them asked if I would be willing to speak at their company sales kick-off meeting in Las Vegas in February. Susan answered for me and said I would be happy to attend.

The party was fun and Susan told me at the end I had done an excellent job promoting the book. As I was leaving, she stopped me and said, "I have a gift for you."

I said, "Oh thank you, I'm sorry I didn't get you one."

"That's okay, this is something I made."

I said, "Oh really!" I was hoping it wasn't food.

"It's my special holiday fruitcake. I think your kids will like it."

I was trying to be cheerful and said, "Thank you! I'm sure they will love it."

She handed me a beautifully wrapped gift box then she turned and walked away. For an instant, I looked for a trash bin to toss it in. I was worried someone might see me so I brought it home.

I carried the cake in and Pam met me at the back door. We kissed and I gave her the box.

I said, "This is a gift from Susan."

"I hope it's not donuts."

"It's a fruitcake."

Pam frowned and asked, "Should we toss it now or risk trying it?"

"It's such a beautiful box and I did haul it home. We should at least sample it."

"Okay, but this may not be a good idea."

I told her how well the party went as she took the cake out and sliced it. She put a slice on a plate and handed it to me.

I said, "Ladies first, please go ahead and try some." I tried to give her the cake back.

She held up her hands and said, "Oh no! I tried the donuts. This time you go first!"

I took the plate and cut off a tiny piece. I sniffed it then took a bite.

"This is good! I'm surprised!"

"You aren't lying to me, are you?"

"No seriously, it's good." I took another bite.

I could tell Pam wasn't sure so she took my fork and took a small bite.

"Wow! It's good!"

Pam cut herself a slice.

She asked, "So the party was successful?"

"It was, and I got invited to speak at a company's kick-off meeting in Las Vegas in February, all expenses paid."

"Wow!"

I said, "Yes, wow! I'm going to have another piece. I also want milk or something to go with it."

"Me too."

We sat in the kitchen, ate some cake, and talked more about the party and my upcoming Las Vegas trip.

CHAPTER 13

THE NEXT WEEK I RECEIVED several copies of the draft. I offered one to Pam but she said she was sticking to her position not to interfere. I gave one to Ricky and one to Sally. Ricky was leaving for an extended trip and said he would let me know his opinion the next weekend. Sally gave me daily reviews on what she read. She liked the book and said the seven rules of marriage were excellent.

On Friday evening, I saw Ricky come home. I gave him some time to settle in then sent a text to him asking if he read the book and if I could come over. He texted back that he had read it but he was tired and asked if I could meet him for breakfast at our favorite restaurant the next morning. He said he'd meet me at 9:00 after his workout.

I was there the next morning, reading the paper and having coffee when he arrived.

I said, "Good morning, Marine." I do a poor salute as I often do when I see him then asked, "Did you do your ten-mile hike with full pack and weapon today?"

"Yes I did, plus I flew up north and chased a few terrorists away from the Canadian border as well."

"You always talk about the Canadian border as if we should build a thirty-foot tall electrified fence there."

"You should listen to me on this. I love the Canadians and especially their hockey and bacon but we have thousands of miles of unguarded border with them. No one knows who's sneaking across."

"So you think the Marines should be guarding our northern border?"

"If the Marines did it, the border would be secure!"

"I would love to continue to discuss border security but I'm hungry, are you ready to order?"

He replied, "Yes, I'm starved."

We ordered and chatted about sports while we waited for the food. Breakfast arrived and we ate.

As we finished I asked him, "Did you like the book?"

He ignored my question and inquired, "Did Pam read it?"

"No, she says she'll wait till it's published. She doesn't think I can handle any critique from her. So did you like it?"

"I did. The stories are entertaining. You counsel some strange people. Now I know why you are who you are."

"That doesn't sound like a compliment."

"It wasn't."

"I thought so."

"Your seven rules are excellent! I know a couple of them you got from me, didn't you?" he asked with pride.

I said, "I'm sorry but I cannot tell who my sources are."

"You don't have to tell me; I know you're stealing a couple of my rules."

"Do I need to list you as a co-writer?" I asked sarcastically.

"Yes."

I said, "I'll have to give that some thought. This is my answer—no. Do you have any other comments on the book?"

"Yes, I didn't know you were so sexist."

"What?" I was surprised.

"That stupid test is sexist."

"My test works."

"I don't care if it works; the test basically says a man should knock the woman in the head with a club and drag her to his cave if she has a job, makes good money, is attractive, cleans the house, and wears thongs."

"It doesn't say that!"

"Maybe I'm paraphrasing a bit. You do say you'll only help a man keep his wife if she has a job, makes good money, is attractive, cleans the house, and wears the right gown or panties to bed. Also, now that I think about it, maybe the test works because it convinces you to work harder for the couple!"

"I use the test to help convince the man he has someone he should focus on and keep."

"Tell yourself whatever you want but I think the test somehow makes you feel more dedicated to the couple so *you* work harder for *them*, not that the man works any harder."

"I don't care what you say, the test works."

"I can see any woman who gets a high score would be worth keeping. Assuming she isn't an axe murderer or drug dealer—and that reminds me of something else I wanted to discuss. You never ask about a woman's arrest record. I would think a woman with multiple felonies should get some points off."

"You have a good point; I should consider adding that."

"One thing I took away is some of the people you counseled were truly broken and you helped them. I was proud of you. You really do make a difference in your counseling. You're a hero to me!"

"Thank you!"

"Let me clarify that. You're a hero like a comic book hero, not a real hero like a Marine or a policeman."

"Gee, I see. I'm like an imaginary comic book hero. Like Superman?"

"No, not Superman! He's cool. I was thinking more like Robin."

I said sarcastically, "I'm like Robin. The guy with no special powers, he's only a sidekick."

"Yeah, you're like Robin. But you don't think Pam should read it now?"

"No, she says she doesn't want to."

"In the test, a woman gets points off for wearing pajamas or sweatpants out in public. I've seen Pam wear pajamas and sweatpants with you to pick up the kids."

"So?"

"You don't get it, do you?"

"Get what?"

"Your wife would get points off for her pajamas, sweatpants, her pets, and maybe even for her panties depending upon what she wears. When she reads this, she'll be pissed at you."

"No she won't."

"Oh yes she will. I also need to tell you something. Brenda wears granny panties."

"Why did you say that? I won't ever be able to forget it! I don't need to know the kind of panties your wife wears."

"Would you agree Brenda is a great-looking woman?"

"I would agree as long as you don't go postal on me."

"I won't but I don't care if she wears granny panties. She must think granny panties are comfortable."

I said, "You miss my point in the book. If a couple is having trouble and the woman doesn't care enough about the man on a romantic weekend to try to make herself appealing to her husband, there's something wrong."

"I got your point but most women won't. You should drop the test. You don't need it."

"The test is a central element of the book."

"Then say you have a test but don't tell the details."

"I can't. It's important to have the details."

"You remember what I said. Women will not like this!"

"No, they'll see what I'm trying to do. They'll support me for trying to get their husbands interested in them."

"The women who score high will like it but the ugly one who is cantankerous, wears camo proudly to church, and believes professional wrestling is a real sport will hate you and the book. There are millions of them and they'll roast you on social media when this book comes out."

I said, "You're underestimating women's intelligence. They'll get what I'm trying to say."

"If you gave points for the woman having to live with some fat redneck who wears nothing but his boxer shorts around the house and drinks beer all day, then yes, they might appreciate what you're trying to say."

"I'm a professional. I know people."

"Okay, Mr. Professional. I can tell that you aren't listening to me and I'm tired of talking about the book. Let's talk about something else."

"Before we do, I have one last question. So did you like the book or not?"

"I liked it and I think it will be a bestseller. I want a signed copy."

"That's good to know."

"The book could be better if you dropped the test."

"No, it stays in."

"I have an old flak jacket in the garage you can use...because you'll need it."

"I won't need it; you're overreacting."

"We'll see."

We normally hang out for a while after breakfast but I was pissed at the Marine. Now my father and my best friend warned me about the test. Of course, I didn't listen.

CHAPTER 14

THE EDITING CONTINUED AND THE plan was for the book to hit the stores on June 1st. Susan was going with me to Las Vegas to speak at a bookseller's annual sales meeting. We were meeting at Chicago O'Hare airport. The flight was at 9:00 AM with boarding at 8:15. I got to the gate at 7:30. Susan was already there and she looked nervous.

"Good morning, how are you?" I asked.

"I hate to fly," she said, ignoring my question.

"Do you? Not me, I love looking out the window. I enjoy seeing the landscape and especially the mountains."

She repeated, "I hate to fly."

The ticket agent interrupted and said over the loudspeaker, "For the flight to Las Vegas, we have had to make a change in equipment. Some of you may be sitting in different seats but everyone will have a seat. Four first-class passengers will be re-seated and will receive a voucher for a future first-class round trip flight."

"Oh no, I hope that's not us!" I said, worried.

"What do you mean not us?" asked Susan.

"We're sitting in the last row of first class. I hope we don't get bumped to coach."

"What do you mean bumped?"

Frustrated at her, I asked, "Didn't you hear the announcement?"

"What announcement? I get overwhelmed at the airport. I try to shut out everything. Is there something wrong?"

The ticket agent made another announcement. "Ms. Fairchild and Dr. Sterling, please step to the counter."

I cursed, "Crap it's us! Let's go to the counter."

We walk to the counter. The ticket agent was a brown-haired, young woman barely out of high school. She smiled wide, the kind of smile where the person seems to have too many teeth. Her teeth were bright white and perfectly straight. Her parents probably spent a fortune on them.

She handed us two boarding passes and two envelopes then said enthusiastically, "I'm sorry but we have to give you seats in coach due to a change in equipment. In each envelope is a voucher for a first-class round-trip flight. You may board with the first-class passengers."

Susan immediately handed hers back and said, "No, that will not do! I have to have a first-class seat."

The agent smiled widely and said in a cheerful tone, "I'm sorry but no first-class seats are available."

Susan said, "Listen to me—I have to have first class. I cannot fly coach. It makes me ill."

The agent smiled less widely with no cheer in her voice and said, "I can get you a first-class seat on a flight tomorrow morning plus you can keep the free ticket."

Susan started to get loud and a little frantic. "Young lady, you are not hearing me! You get someone else in first class to take coach. Not me!"

People started to watch Susan. The agent stopped smiling and said, "Lady, you want on this flight then here is your ticket or you can wait till tomorrow. I have to board this flight; you decide what you want to do." The ticket agent left to board passengers.

I said, "Susan, let's take these seats, we will be okay."

"No! I have to sit in first class. I'm going to get a person in first class to switch seats with me."

Susan walked away from the ticket counter to the boarding area. She shouted, "Attention everyone in first class, I have a seat in coach but I would like to make a trade. I have a free flight voucher for a future flight and I will give you $100 in cash!"

It's a long flight to Vegas from Chicago and it looked like mostly business travelers in first class except for one older woman. No one was interested.

Susan approached the older woman and asked, "Would you please trade seats with me?"

The older woman said, "No."

"Please!"

"Stop bothering me!" said the older woman.

Susan was now desperate. She shouted, "This is my last offer. I will give you $200 plus the free flight voucher."

No one was interested. Susan looked at the older woman again but she turned her head. You could tell people were concerned about her behavior. I could see the ticket agents looking at her and talking quietly.

I tried to calm her down. "Susan, no one wants to trade. If you don't calm down, they'll take you off this flight. Don't worry, we will be fine. We have an aisle and a window. Which one do you want?"

"The window," she growled.

"Crap!" I said to myself. I wanted the window.

We boarded and when we got to our seats, Susan pushed the attendant call button. A young, overly tanned, thin male attendant with blond hair cut in a kewpie doll style came to the seat.

He asked in an irritated and nasally tone, "How may I help you?"

Susan said, "I need a Bloody Mary now!"

"I'm sorry but this is coach and you can buy one after we take off but not now."

"I was supposed to be in first class and due to your airline's incompetence, I got bumped to coach. I should still get first-class service. I want get a free drink now so go get it!"

The attendant said sternly, "You're sitting in coach and coach passengers do not have drinks before takeoff and the drink will not be free. I will be back after takeoff for drinks for all coach passengers."

The attendant left. Susan fumed and mumbled loudly. The longer she sat there the louder she got. I decided to go to the first-class attendant and beg for a drink. I walked up front and explained the situation to the flight attendant. She understood and immediately helped me. I brought the drink back, thinking I had done a good thing.

Susan didn't say anything; she took the drink and drank it quickly. She handed back the glass and said, "I need another one."

I said, "You can wait!"

"No I can't. I need another drink!"

She reached for the attendant button and I blocked her hand.

I said, "Okay, okay! I will beg for another one."

I went back and asked the attendant for another one. I felt awful doing it. She gave me the look of complete indignation and I apologized profusely. She quickly mixed the drink and said there would be no more.

I got back and gave the drink to Susan. I said, "Drink this one slowly because the attendant said there will be no more drinks until we get in the air."

Susan seemed satisfied for the moment. The flight was filling up and the middle seat between us was open. I was praying no one would be in it but I wasn't so lucky. Two people were coming down the aisle, a small Asian man and a large woman. The large woman's hips touched the seats on each side of the aisle as she walked. I prayed, *Please, please let it be the small guy!*

The Asian man passed by. The large woman stopped at our row. I looked up at her. She was wearing a bright blue, loose-fitting dress with a floral pattern. I stood up to let her in.

Susan looked up at the woman and quickly put her armrest down.

The woman said to her, "I can't sit there if the armrest is down. Can you please put it up?"

Susan looked directly at her and said, "No! Why didn't you get a first-class seat, they're bigger!"

"It's too expensive."

"So I have to be punished because you're cheap?"

"Are you going to put the armrest up?"

"No!" Susan said loud and firm.

The woman pushed the call attendant button.

The same male attendant returned and said in an even more nasally voice, "You have to take your seats! We need to push back from the gate."

The woman pointed to Susan's armrest and said, "I need to have the armrest up or I won't fit."

The attendant asked Susan, "Could you please put the armrest up?"

Susan said, "No! I don't want a four-hour flight with a fat woman in my lap."

The attendant said to the woman, "She doesn't have to put the armrest up if she doesn't want to. I know it's rude but there's nothing I can do."

The woman said to the attendant, "I need a different seat."

The attendant said, "Look around! The flight is full!"

"I will not sit next to her if she won't help a person in need," the woman said.

Susan said, "What you need is to lose about 200 pounds."

"That is an awful thing to say," the woman said as she glared at Susan.

The attendant tried to calm them down. "Ladies please, let's remain civil here."

I wanted to get going so I said, "Let me sit in the middle and you can take the aisle. The aisle might be more comfortable for you."

The woman said, "Will you leave the armrest up?"

I grimaced and said, "Sure."

Now everyone was happy but me. You would think the woman or the attendant would have said thanks or something but they didn't say a word. I get into the middle seat and then the woman squeezed into the aisle seat. Susan was right: a large part of the woman was now in my lap.

Susan bent over, looked at the woman and me, then asked, "Are you comfy?"

I whispered, "It's a little tight."

Susan chuckled. "If you think it's tight now, wait an hour. You'll feel like sardine in a can."

"I'll be fine."

"No you won't; you're going to have a terrible trip."

A flight attendant came on the speaker and reminded everyone to buckle his or her seatbelts. The woman tried to buckle her belt but couldn't. She laid it across her stomach and put her arms over it. It looked buckled. Susan saw what she was doing and started to push the call button. I pushed her hand away.

She said in a loud whisper, "It's not safe! She should have to wear a seatbelt like everyone else!"

I whispered back, "Let's not have another scene please. Let the flight attendants handle it, it's their job to check."

"Yeah right, like anyone could see under all that."

"*Susan!*"

"Okay! Okay!"

Susan sat back in her seat and sipped on her Bloody Mary. We got ready to take off. Two flight attendants came by checking for seatbelts. I thought for sure the woman would be caught but she had so many folds and bulges that the seatbelt looked buckled. Susan was busy looking out the window and forgot about the belt.

After takeoff, the woman was restless and was having trouble being still. She kept wiggling around. She crossed and uncrossed her arms over her ample chest several times, apparently looking for a position that was comfortable for her but always uncomfortable for me. Each time she moved her left arm it raked across my chest. Finally, she decided to cross her arms. This put her left elbow across part of my chest. She seemed to like that position and settled in.

Ten minutes later, the woman leaned her seat back. Now her arm drug across my chest and was directly in my ribs. I leaned my seat back too to get her arm out of my ribs. She looked at me and grunted as if she didn't like what I did. I kept the seat back.

Within a few minutes, the woman was asleep. As she fell into a deep sleep, she shifted her weight more toward me and away from the aisle. I felt squashed. I leaned toward Susan.

Susan said, "Oh no, you don't! You aren't taking any of my seat!" She pushed me back.

I then tried to push the woman gently away from me, but she wouldn't budge. I was miserable.

A few minutes passed and Susan said, "I need you to get me another drink. I'm starting to feel anxious again."

I said firmly, "There's no way I can get out of this seat."

I turned and tried to look back as best as I could. I saw that the attendants were getting the drink carts ready.

I said, "I can see a drink cart. It will be here in a few minutes."

Susan said, "If they don't get here soon, I'm climbing out!"

Thankfully, the drink cart came quickly and Susan stocked up. She ordered two and I ordered two. One for me and an extra one for Susan in case the cart didn't come back around again.

Two hours into the flight, Susan was calm after three drinks. She was sipping on the fourth. I was reading when suddenly the woman's arms slowly unfolded from her chest. Her left arm fell into my lap and her hand was between my legs. Her right arm flopped into the aisle.

Susan saw where the woman's hand was. She smiled and asked, "Are you two planning to have some fun? Do you want a blanket so you two can cuddle up?"

I glared at Susan. I gently picked up the woman's hand and pushed her arm back. Suddenly, she started to list toward the aisle. Her body poured over the aisle armrest and now her right arm extended well into the aisle. The people walking in the aisle had to turn sideways to get through. The woman laid that way for ten minutes or so. She didn't move during that period and she seemed to have stopped breathing. I began to wonder if she was dead and so did other people.

Someone must have told the attendant because he came and looked at her closely. He said to me, "I don't think she's breathing!"

I looked at the woman. She looked perfectly still. The attendant bent over close to her then said, "I don't see her chest moving."

People from nearby rows all turned to see what was going on. Susan had been watching and said loudly, "When we land I want to see how you are going to get her out of the seat!"

The attendant said, "Please keep your voice down! I don't want to frighten the other passengers."

Susan said in a loud voice, "I think you're going to need a crane."

I said in a low voice, "Susan, please be quiet!"

The attendant bent down to the woman and asked softly, "Are you okay?"

The woman didn't respond.

The attendant gently touched her arm. "Are you okay?"

The woman woke up in a start and screamed, "Why are you touching me?"

The shocked attendant jumped back and said, "I thought you were dead!"

"I'm not dead! I was asleep! I've just come from Europe and I'm exhausted."

"You didn't seem to be breathing. I'm sorry to bother you. May I get you anything?"

"No! Don't bother me anymore, I want to sleep."

The attendant was more than embarrassed and quickly walked back to the back. Susan laughed and said in a slurred voice, "This has been my best flight ever!"

I said sarcastically, "Yeah, it's been great for me too."

The woman was soon asleep again and my misery continued. She alternated between sleeping on me and laying into the aisle.

By the time we got close to Las Vegas, Susan had finished six drinks. She wanted another one but the flight attendant refused to give her any more. She was feeling great.

An attendant announced we were on approach to Las Vegas. Susan was watching the large woman closely and saw she had not buckled her seatbelt. Before I could stop her, she pushed the call button.

The male attendant arrived again. He said, "This is my favorite row. What now?"

Susan pointed to the woman and said, "She didn't buckle her belt."

The attendant asked the woman, "Could you please buckle your seatbelt?"

"It won't fit."

"Where's your belt extender?"

"I don't have one."

The attendant was shocked and asked, "You didn't have one for takeoff?"

"No, I forgot to ask for one."

The attendant rolled his eyes and groaned. "Geez, let me see if I can find another one. I think we gave out the ones we had."

The attendant walked quickly down the aisle to the back. The big woman bent over and said to Susan, "Tattle tale!"

Susan stuck her tongue out at her.

The woman said, "That's childish!"

The woman looked at me and asked, "Is she your girlfriend?"

I said, "Never, ever."

The attendant came back and said, "I can't find one. You should have told us before we took off. We could have easily have gotten another one. The FAA rules are clear about this."

"I'm sorry," said the woman.

The attendant said, "Use your arms and lean against the seat in front of you."

Susan interjected, "If we crash, the guy in front of her is going to be a pancake. I can't believe the seat was designed for this!"

"Susan, you aren't being helpful!" I said.

She replied, "I'm just saying no seat can hold that back."

The woman leaned against the seat. Luckily, the landing was fine. For me it was my worst flight ever, I had a headache from dealing with Susan, and my back ached from not being able to move much during the trip.

The plane stopped at the gate and the large woman quickly stood up. I got up and stood behind her in the aisle to stretch.

Susan said in a loud voice, "I have to go pee." Everyone around heard her and they started to snicker.

I said, "We will be off the plane soon."

"I have to go pee now!" she said loudly.

I asked, "Why didn't you go when we were in the air?"

"I can't pee in those putrid, bacteria infested rooms. Plus, I couldn't get around that bulk," she said, shooting a last look of indignation at the fat woman. "I have to go now!"

She got into the aisle and pushed past the large woman and several first-class passengers. She bolted off the plane to the airport restroom. I had to carry her bags and mine. I waited for ten minutes outside the bathroom.

Finally, she came out and said, "I want to see the Luke Bryan show. I think he's so cute. I want to squeeze his behind."

I laughed and said, "His show isn't till tonight and it's only mid-day here."

"I want to go now!"

"Go ahead."

She was drunk and I was tired of her antics so I let her go on her own. She left with her bags to go to the show. I saw her the next morning at my speech and she acted as if nothing happened the day before. The speech went well and the audience enjoyed my stories. At the end, Susan came up on stage and announced the book would hit the stores on June 1. Susan had gotten a well-known book critic to provide a positive pre-release review. She read the review to the audience. The buzz at the meeting about the book was tremendous.

Susan and I were supposed to fly back together after the meeting but I took a later flight without telling her. I wanted a peaceful trip.

CHAPTER 15

After the Las Vegas trip, the rush was on to complete the editing. We had a deadline to make in order to be ready for the summer season. We were all working hard to get it finished and patience was running a little thin.

In two meetings with Susan and Mike there were big arguments on the final wording. Carla twice had to referee shouting matches between them. The good Susan was long gone and the bad Susan had to have her way on everything. I could see clearly now why Mike hated Susan at the end of each book. She kept asking me for new stories to add but Mike was pushing hard for Susan to wrap it up.

Carla called me and said Mike and Susan wanted to meet with me on a Wednesday morning in March for one last editing session. I got to the office and as usual, Carla was waiting for me at the elevator. She was wearing a lovely dark blue suit.

I said, "Good morning Carla. I love your suit. Do you get a clothing allowance? You always wear the nicest clothes."

"Thank you! I wish I got a clothing allowance. I'm addicted to clothes. Now, I need to warn you, Susan was now making cupcakes. They look good but our network guy was out of the office yesterday afternoon. The entire office is waiting for his post. Hopefully he wasn't poisoned; I know he tried one yesterday morning."

Susan was on the phone when I entered. Mike was looking at his cell phone.

Susan said to the person on the phone, "I understand how you feel but this isn't working out for me." She then listened.

Mike pointed to his ring finger on his left hand and then shook his head. I took it to mean she was talking to her fiancé.

She said, "Yes, I will help you pay for half of the wedding deposits."

She listened for a few seconds.

"No, I will not return the ring. You knew that was in our prenuptial agreement!"

She listened for a few seconds.

"That's fine, you know my attorney; go ahead and call him. He will tell you there is no chance of getting it back."

She listened for a few more seconds, then said, "Don't call me anymore!"

She hung up, turned around and said, "You two ready to get started?"

Mike said, "I'm ready."

I was surprised at what happened and said, "We couldn't help but overhear your conversation. Do you need a few minutes?"

"No, I'm fine."

"Are you sure?" I asked.

She replied quickly in a condescending tone, "When I need therapy, I'll call you and make an appointment."

I ignored her reply and said, "Susan, I know ending an engagement is one of the top ten most stressful things a person can undergo. It's not like we break off engagements often."

Mike laughed, "You don't know Susan!"

Susan glared at him and said, "You keep quiet!"

Mike smiled then reached up and motioned as if he zipped his lips.

I asked, "How long was the engagement?"

She replied, "Six months."

Mike blurted out, "Six months! That's a record for you!"

"Damn you, Mike! Stay out of this!"

Mike shot back, "You intentionally had me sit here while you ended another engagement and you expect me to be quiet?"

"I didn't intentionally do that. He was calling from Europe and this was the only time I could talk to him."

"I bet," countered Mike.

I asked, "Why are you breaking up?"

"He's an immature jerk who is never going to grow up!"

Mike interjected, "That's not the reason! I bet you ended it because he started to ask questions you don't like to answer."

She countered vehemently, "No, you're wrong! I ended it because he's not the one for me."

"Baloney, that's not the reason. You ended ours—"

"Don't you dare go there!" she interrupted. She quickly looked at me then turned back to Mike.

Mike looked at me and said, "I see. Ed doesn't know, does he?"

Susan pleaded, "Mike, please don't bring this up."

"Ed should know about this. Susan and I were engaged for five months."

I was surprised because I had never seen one bit of affection between them.

"You ended our engagement abruptly when I asked a couple of questions about your health and what you intended to do about it."

"Damn you, Mike, that's not why!"

"Yes it was. I remember exactly where we were and what I asked. We were fine until then. Do you remember what I asked?"

Susan replied angrily, "Yes, I remember!"

"Did you call him Bobby like you did me several times?"

She hissed, "Mike, don't talk about Bobby!"

"I bet you did. Bobby has been gone for ten years. He's dead and not coming back."

"I know that!"

Mike yelled back, "No you don't! Until you let him go completely, you will never get any better and no man will ever measure up. Those damn rings you keep are a shrine to him."

Susan screamed, "Don't talk about my rings or Bobby!" She started to sob.

Carla rushed in and said, "Stop it! Stop it! We never talk about Bobby. Mike, you know the rules! Now you go downstairs with Ed, get some coffee, and cool off!"

Carla went over to Susan and put her arms around her. Mike and I got up, walked to the elevator, and went to a coffee shop in the lobby. We ordered coffee and sat at a table.

Mike said apologetically, "I'm sorry you heard that."

"You two have a much longer and deeper history than I knew."

"Yes, we do."

"Tell me about it. It sometimes helps to talk to someone who doesn't know the details."

"Susan and I met here in Chicago after college. We wanted to be writers. She worked for a newspaper and I was a bartender full time. I met her at the bar. I fell in love with her immediately. I asked her to marry me at least a dozen times but she always said no. A friend of mine since childhood, Bobby Hampton, came to a party with me and met Susan. Bobby was tall, handsome, and athletic. He was a lieutenant in the Navy reserves and wanted to be a Naval aviator. He tried but washed out as an aviator. After six years in the Navy, he went back to school and got his law degree. The night they met, he was wearing his Navy dress uniform. Susan loves a man in uniform and she fell hard for him."

Mike took a drink of his coffee then continued. "Bobby at first wasn't interested in Susan because he knew I loved her. However, she pursued him. After a couple of months, he knew my relationship with her wasn't going anywhere and he asked if he could see her. I reluctantly agreed and they were soon engaged. Even though he couldn't be an aviator, Bobby loved to fly and he had a small plane. They planned an engagement party in upper Michigan for a weekend in late May. Susan, Bobby, and I were planning to fly together to Mackinac on a Thursday but Susan couldn't make it. Bobby and I flew up north to meet some friends. I decided to stay in Mackinac and he flew back alone on

Saturday morning to get her. He never made it back to Chicago. He crashed into Lake Michigan, west of Muskegon. The weather was bad and it took a long time for the Coast Guard to arrive. They found the plane but they never found Bobby. I told her about the accident and of course, she took it badly. Since Bobby, she has had six engagements. One of them was to me."

"Why does she keep the rings?"

"Bobby gave her a nice ring that he bought from his uncle's jewelry store on Mackinac Island in Michigan. The engagement ring had a minor problem and Bobby had his uncle repair the ring while we were there. He had the ring with him when he went down."

"I see. She has an emotional attachment to the rings."

"Yes she does. She kept mine, which pissed me off and it still does."

"Do you still love her?"

"Yes but each time we do a book, I love her a little less. As you know, there are two Susans. I fell in love with the good Susan. Her condition worsened after Bobby's death. I ignored the strange things I saw her do and asked her to marry me anyway. I thought she just had a few quirks. One Saturday at the end of our engagement, she had a particularly bad day. It was Bobby's birthday. I asked her at dinner that night about her condition and if she needed help. I just wanted her to get better. She freaked out and the next day she broke off our engagement over the phone just like today. The bad Susan is here more and more. I have a hard time dealing with the bad version. When I saw her this morning, I knew it was going to be hard day."

"Maybe we shouldn't work on the book today."

"No, you'll see she will be fine when we get back. I mean fine for the bad Susan."

"How long do we stay here?"

"Carla will text me when Susan's ready. I've had to come here many times in the past to let Susan cool off or to rest."

"Carla told me to never talk about her fiancé or her relationships."

Mike said, "I know the rule too but sometimes I get angry about the situation. She breaks off an engagement right in front of me and it brought back all the emotions I felt when she did it to me."

"Why has she had so many engagements?"

"I believe her relationships fail for two reasons: her health and because she hasn't let Bobby go. After our engagement ended, she started looking for a Bobby replacement. Since we work together often, I have met each one. All her boyfriends are the same. They are young men, twenty-five to thirty years old, handsome, athletic, arrogant, and immature like Bobby was."

"Bobby was immature even after being in the Navy?"

"Oh yes! He was immature, arrogant, hot-headed, and a risk taker. He didn't make it as an aviator because he wouldn't follow the rules. He thought he could make his own rules. The weather forecast was awful the day he wanted to leave Mackinac for Chicago. I grew up in Mackinac and I know how bad the weather can be there. I went flying with him in bad weather before. He scared the crap out of me a couple of times. I would only fly with him when the weather forecast was good. I would check the forecast myself because he would lie about it. The weather forecast was the reason why I didn't go. Bobby took off anyway."

"Does Susan see a therapist?"

"Oh yes, she has seen many. One of her issues is that she blames herself for Bobby having the accident. She didn't fly up with us because of work. She believes if she had focused on him and not her job that he would still be alive."

"Have you ever seen any improvement in her condition?"

"Yes, when she takes her medication she gets better, but she hates taking it."

His phone buzzed and he looked at it. He said, "Susan is ready."

We finished our coffee and went back upstairs. Carla was standing next to Susan, who was in her chair. Without any mention about what happened earlier, Susan said, "Now I want to review the story on the couple from Wisconsin. I've heard of men having multiple wives but I haven't heard of a woman having multiple husbands. Ed, tell me more about it."

I said, "The woman owned two large farms in Wisconsin. She grew up as the only child of a dairy farmer. Her grandfather died when she was in her early twenties and left her his farm. When she took over the farm, the dairy business across the country was bad. Milk prices were down and many farmers were getting out of the business. Luckily for her, the farm she inherited was debt free and the farm was profitable. She fell in love with a young man who was the farm foreman. They got engaged. They were almost ready to marry when her father died in a car accident. She inherited another farm. The foreman of her father's farm was an old boyfriend. She started traveling back and forth between the two farms. She soon discovered she loved both men and she didn't know what to do. The farms were three hours apart and since the towns were small communities of mostly farmers, she decided to marry both men."

Carla asked, "Is that legal?"

"No it's not. She told the men what she was going to do and if they didn't go along it, she would end the relationship and they would be out of a job. The economy was terrible then and the men felt trapped. Being submissive men, they agreed to her plan. The men knew of each other but never met. She would spend three to four days with each husband. The woman had children with each man. This went on for years until one of her sons became aware of the situation. The seventeen-year-old son wanted to meet the other children. The families got together and jealousies soon developed between the men. They became competitive and wanted the woman to pick one to live with. The three of them came to me for counseling. Needless to say, it was a circus trying to resolve their issues."

Carla asked in an incredulous voice, "Why did she want to deal with two men? I have trouble dealing with one."

Everyone laughed.

I said, "In the beginning, the woman felt she needed both men. She loved her grandfather's farm and her father's farm; she felt the only way to keep both farms was to have them married to her. Over time she emotionally dominated the two men."

Mike asked, "How did it end?"

"Both men loved her and were dependent on her financially since she was the sole owner of both farms. They had signed strict prenuptial contracts that prevented the men from owning any part of the farms. The authorities became aware of the situation and they forced her to pick one husband or she would go to jail. She divorced the second man she married."

"I'm surprised the authorities didn't prosecute her," said Mike.

I said, "That was the big worry but the authorities decided not to press charges once she divorced the second husband."

Susan said, "I suppose none of them are together now."

"No, she is still married to the first husband but she doesn't live with the other man anymore. She still travels back and forth to the farms. I have met the children and they have all adjusted to having stepbrothers and sisters."

"How did you help them?" Susan asked.

"Mostly, I focused on making the two men stronger. They needed to establish boundaries they could live with. The second man, with my help, left the farm and found a new job. He hasn't remarried yet but he has started to date. I see him one on one still."

We decided the story would be included in the book and worked the rest of the day on editing it. That was the only time Carla ever stayed with us. I guess she wanted to make sure Susan was okay. I left the meeting with homework to do. I worked hard the next two weeks to get Susan what she wanted.

We made the deadline and the book was ready. There is always a party when a book is finished. I went to the party but Mike didn't show. Carla said he had left for a Caribbean vacation. The good Susan—who I hadn't seen in a while—was there. I felt a big sense of accomplishment and relief but Susan warned me. She said only the first half of the game was over. She told me to rest up and enjoy the halftime because the second half, which was promoting the book, would be rough. She was right.

CHAPTER 16

PAM'S DAD ASKED HER TO come to Tucson, Arizona a week before the book tour started because her mother was ill. The summer is a lighter time for Pam at work, so we packed up with the kids and headed to Arizona. Rebecca stayed home with Sunny and the birds. I was about to start the book tour and I wanted to see Pam's mother now in case her health worsened. When we arrived, Pam pitched in helping her mother, Flora, and I took care of the kids.

Her parents live in a remote, desert community west of Tucson. I have always admired Pam's father, Carl, who is an amazing man. Carl didn't have much formal education but he is a mechanical genius. He can build or repair anything.

Carl and Flora's home in the desert is simple but beautiful. Especially the way he landscaped the property with colorful desert plants and cacti. They live a quiet life there with no Internet and only two TV channels that aren't always clear.

I loved going there not only because of the desert's beauty but because it was easy for me to pursue my passion for dirt biking. In Arizona, there are endless places to dirt bike. I can put on a helmet, leave my father-in-law's garage, and in five minutes be on a long trail with nothing but lizards and roadrunners to bother me.

I learned to dirt bike on my grandfather's farm in Michigan. He lived near some sand dunes where I hung out as a kid. When we were dating, I took Pam there. As much as I loved to dirt bike the dunes, she never warmed up to it. She didn't ride, didn't want to learn, and going there to watch me ride wasn't thrilling for her. She especially lost interest in it when she saw a kid on a dirt bike get hurt in an accident. She feels dirt bikes are dangerous and tries her best to keep me off them. Somehow, though, I convinced Pam to allow me to buy a bike and leave it with her parents. We usually go to Arizona a week or two each year and I spend as much time as I can on the bike. She said she would rather I have a bike in the Arizona desert than have one in the crowded streets of Chicago.

Whenever we visit Tucson, we always go as a family up to Mount Lemmon, which is in the Coronado National Forest. It's a beautiful area on top of a 9,000-foot mountain north of Tucson. We go there and picnic because the views are gorgeous and the kids can run around.

On the morning of the trip to Mount Lemmon, Pam's mother wasn't feeling well so I decided to take the kids myself. The girls were excited about going and I loved going there. We left early in the morning.

To get to the top of Mount Lemmon, you can travel up like most of the tourists do—on a modern, safe, paved road. The other way is how the dirt bikers and folks with four-wheel trucks get there, up the backside of the mountain. I had always wanted to go up the backside but Pam was always reluctant because she liked the easy tourist drive. That morning, I decided to try it.

It was a beautiful morning for a drive. There was a clear blue sky with no clouds in sight. It would be hot in the desert but cool up on the mountain. Natalie and Gracie were in the back seat with headphones and books.

As I got to the backside road, I expected to see a large sign pointing the way to Mount Lemmon but there was only a small county sign with a road name. It looked like they don't want many people to take this route. For a second, I thought I should take the tourist road but I wanted some adventure. I had a new rental SUV so I turned off the main road with confidence that we would be fine.

The road was paved and smooth; I made good time. I thought I had been worried for no reason. After several miles of good road, there was a large sign that said the paved road would end in a mile. The paved road ended but the road was gravel and in good shape. I slowed down some. A few miles later there was another sign; it said: "Road no longer maintained by county." I thought if it got too bad, I would turn around.

A mile later the road started to get rough; I had to slow down significantly. The girls were now bouncing around in the back and loving it. I worried that I was going to kill the rental car on the bad road.

Another mile farther and I was barely crawling along. We came around a bend and in the middle of the road was a big buck with a large set of antlers. I stopped the car. The girls squealed when they saw him. The buck was standing perfectly still; he was staring at something in the road.

Between the buck and our car was the biggest rattlesnake I have ever seen. The snake stretched across the road. It had to be nearly six feet long and was thicker than my arm. The snake had caught a bird, mouse, or something and was eating it. The girls were excited and squealing about the snake and the buck. The buck didn't want to go back where it came but it didn't want to get too close to the snake. The snake was taking its time having breakfast so the buck and I waited.

The buck started to get restless. We were in an open area, which isn't healthy for a big buck. I didn't know if it was hunting season but I wouldn't have been surprised if somebody shot at it.

The buck edged closer to the snake. The snake immediately coiled up. The buck crept past the snake and the snake's rattles were going wild.

Finally, the buck got past the snake then ran past the car up a trail and disappeared. The buck was so close to the car we could have easily touched him. I edged the car to the side of the road to get away from the snake. I had my window down and you could hear the snake's rattles. The girls had unbuckled their belts and gotten up. Gracie was hiding on the floor but Natalie pressed her face up against the window looking at the snake. We edged past the snake and started crawling up the road again.

A few minutes down the road, Natalie said, "Dad, I have to go pee. I got excited when I saw the snake and now I have to go bad."

I said, "Nattie, we will be on top soon and there is a bathroom there."

She said, "Okay."

The reality was I had no idea how far we were from the top. The road was now a steep, narrow, winding incline and full of small boulders that often scraped the bottom of the car. The mountain was on one side of the car and a steep cliff on the other. We were barely crawling along. I tried to get Natalie to take her mind off having to go to the bathroom by having her look for animals and birds. A few minutes passed and we were still not at the top.

Natalie said, "Dad, I really have to go."

"If I stop can you go on the side of the road?"

Natalie said with horror on her face, "Daddy, there are snakes out there!"

"I will check to make sure there are no snakes and I will protect you."

She said, "Okay, because I have to go right now."

Gracie said, "Me too."

We stopped. I got out and made sure nothing was around. I opened the passenger back door and she got out. I stood with my back turned. Natalie went first, then Gracie.

Once they got back in the car, Gracie was excited and said, "I never peed outside before."

Natalie said, "Me neither. Daddy, do you think Mommy will be mad to hear we did that?"

I said, "I don't want to think about that right now."

It was now close to noon and if we had taken the modern road, we would be safe and eating lunch on top of the mountain. The road was now nothing but boulders of all sizes. I had to edge my way past a few large ones.

We went around a bend and I stopped. The road was washed out so much in the middle that there was only a rock ledge path on either side of the car. I got out and examined the road. I decided the tires would fit on the two ledges.

I started to inch the car up the road. The car went a hundred feet or so, then there was a high point with several large boulders in the middle of the road. I thought the car would clear it.

I edged the car over the rocks but suddenly I heard a large thud from underneath the car and the vehicle stopped moving. I got out. The front tires were a couple inches off the ground…and so were the back tires. The car was teetering back and forth on the boulders.

I told the girls, "We're stuck."

The girls weren't scared but excited; Gracie started yelling, "We're stuck! We're stuck."

Natalie said, "We can push if you like. We once helped Mommy push our car when we got stuck in the snow!"

I said, "We'll see. Let me look at this first."

I needed to get weight in the front in order for the tires to touch. I asked the girls to pile in the front seat, which they immediately did. It helped, but not enough. I took small boulders from the road and put them on the front floorboard. Now the car was tipping forward. The tires had traction and we inched forward.

"We're moving!" said Gracie.

"Way to go, Dad!" yelled Natalie.

I slowly edged the car off the boulders then stopped. The road ahead looked even rockier.

I sat in the car, thinking about what to do. I didn't know how much farther it was to the top and it was a long, scary trip back.

I asked the girls, "Do we turn back or try to go forward?"

Natalie said, "This is fun. Let's go ahead."

"Yes Daddy, go ahead," said Gracie enthusiastically.

I edged forward with rocks tearing at the bottom of the car. We rounded a bend and we were at the top. We had made it.

Natalie said, "Can we go back home to Grandpa's the way we came? It was fun!"

I said, "I don't know, we'll see." There was no way I was going back down the backside.

We had lunch. The girls ran around and tired themselves out. After three hours at the top, we got in the car for the trip back.

I told the girls, "Now, girls, when we get back, Mom is going to ask you about your day. Let's not talk about being stuck on the road today. You should never tell a lie but at times we shouldn't talk about certain things."

Gracie said, "Like peeing on the rocks."

"Yes that's right. Do you understand?"

"Yes, Daddy," they said.

We drove down the normal, safe way. Once we were off the mountain, the girls fell asleep. It was twilight when we got back. When I pulled into the driveway, Pam was waiting on the front porch. The girls jumped from the car and sprinted to her.

Pam asked, "Did you have a good time?"

Both girls were excited; Natalie said, "It was exciting! We saw this huge deer with big antlers and a large rattlesnake in the road eating something."

Pam said, "Wow! Gracie, how was your day?"

Gracie said, "I peed outside and so did sister."

Pam smiled and said, "You did?"

Gracie said, "Yes. Sister and I had to pee. Daddy let us pee on the road. I want to do it again."

Natalie said, "Gracie, you're saying too much, remember what we talked about with Daddy?"

Pam looked at me then asked Gracie, "What else are you not supposed to tell Mommy?"

Gracie said, "We got stuck in the road! It was fun and scary."

Pam said, "What?"

Gracie said, "Yes, and Daddy had to put rocks in the car."

Pam frowned and said to me, "You went up the backside, didn't you?"

I grimaced and said, "Yes."

Pam stared at me and said, "We'll talk later."

I knew I was in the doghouse again. You can never trust a four-year-old to stay quiet.

CHAPTER 17

On Sunday, Pam and the girls took me to the airport to fly to Los Angeles for my first TV interview for the book tour. At the curb, we said our goodbyes.

"Now here is the list of things you need to do every day. I made several copies because I know you will lose at least one." Pam handed me an envelope.

"Thanks for this! I don't want to get in trouble with you if I forget something."

Pam said, "On the drive in, I remembered another item. Did you tell your parents about the book yet?"

"Not yet. I'll give them a call."

"Okay, but add it to the list right away."

"I will."

I kissed the girls. "I will see you soon. You two obey Mommy, okay?"

"Yes Daddy," they replied.

I kissed Pam and said, "I love you and I'll talk to you soon."

"I love you too. Please be careful."

I gathered my bags and walked into the terminal. I hurried to security and there was a long line. I finally got to the gate only to find there was a gate change. I barely made the flight. Somewhere from the curb through security and to a new gate, I lost the envelope with Pam's to-do list. I had lost them before and survived so I didn't worry about it.

Susan met me in Los Angeles. The book hit the stores on Friday and Susan said it was selling well. In the Sunday edition of a Los Angeles paper, there was a great review of the book. The timing of the review was a perfect way to start the tour.

Anna Carson, a well-known female TV personality, was going to interview me on a Monday morning local broadcast. Anna was an up-and-coming personality rumored to be the next anchor on a nationwide morning news program. She was a pretty, intelligent, and charming blonde in her mid-thirties. Susan had prepped her producers on the book.

I had never been on television and I was nervous but Susan was even more so. I was in the makeup chair and she was prepping me for the twentieth time.

Susan said, "Remember to look at Anna and not the camera."

"Yes, I know."

"Look at her eyes, nothing else."

"Yes, I know."

"I don't care if she gets naked, look at her eyes."

"Yes, I know."

"Remember to smile."

"Yes, I know."

"Don't talk too fast. Pause after each sentence."

"Yes, I know."

"You think you're funny but you aren't. Don't make any jokes."

"Yes, I know."

"If you are thirsty, you must drink now. I don't want you to spill water or choke during the interview."

"I'm not thirsty."

"You know the questions she will ask so answer them exactly like we practiced."

"I will."

"Are you ready?"

"Yes."

"Now don't screw up! The national network producers will be watching. If you do well, they'll want you on their shows."

I asked, "If I pee in my pants will that be a problem?"

With an alarmed look on her face, she said, "Do you have to pee? Because if you do, go now."

"No, I'm kidding."

Susan said, "Don't joke! I'm too nervous for any joking!"

A producer came in and said, "Dr. Sterling, you will be on in three minutes. Please follow me to the set."

I followed the producer along with Susan. On the set were two armchairs and a coffee table with a large vase of flowers. I sat down and a technician adjusted my microphone then he left. I hadn't met Anna yet but she was nearby reading her notes. There was a scenic view of Los Angeles in the windows behind me.

She finished reading, sat down beside me then reached out her hand and said, "Dr. Sterling, it's a pleasure to meet you. I'm Anna Carson."

I shook her hand and replied with a smile, "It's a pleasure to meet you, Mrs. Carson."

"Please call me Anna."

The producer said, "In five seconds, we will be on."

I sat on the chair praying not to do something stupid.

Anna looked at the camera and said, "Well, we are back and now I have the pleasure of talking to Dr. Ed Sterling. Dr. Sterling is the author of the book, *Flannel Gowns and Granny Panties*, which is getting great reviews. The book is about helping people in their marriages."

She held the book up to the camera and said, "I love the cover! It really catches your eye! Dr. Sterling is a marriage counselor and you practice in Chicago, correct?"

I felt relieved she was following the script I had practiced.

"Yes, I have been in practice in Chicago for the past twelve years."

"I found the stories of your counseling stories to be hilarious. Are these stories really true?"

"Yes, the stories are true but I have changed the names and places where the couples live to protect their identity."

"The Sterling Seven Rules for keeping your marriage strong are insightful and I could see they could be of help to couples. Do you use them in your counseling?"

"Yes, the rules are my foundational stones for counseling."

I was starting to relax and was smiling.

Anna smiled and said, "Dr. Sterling doesn't like granny panties. Now for the men in the audience, these are cotton, usually white panties that fully cover a woman's bottom and go up to the waist. They are comfortable to wear but not sexy. Now, why don't you like a woman to wear granny panties?"

This question wasn't in the script. I tensed up a bit. Where are the questions on my family that were supposed to come next? I thought fast.

"Couples come to me when their marriage is in trouble. I try to diagnose what's going on in the marriage. I ask the couple many questions. One question I ask the man is, 'Does your wife wear granny panties on a romantic getaway?'"

Anna asked pointedly, "Why do you ask about a woman's panties?"

"If a couple is having trouble, I think a woman should try to make herself appealing to her husband. Men don't think granny panties are sexy."

"What if I told you I wear them? Do you think I wouldn't be appealing to my husband in granny panties?"

I was trying to think fast. I said, "Anna, you're an intelligent, beautiful, and successful woman. If you and your husband came to me for counseling, I would help him to understand what he would be missing if he lost you. I try to make a man with a good woman realize what he has and to try to keep her. Too many men fail to see what is right in front of them. I'm sure I would counsel your husband that you're an absolute angel and he should make you happy at all costs."

Anna's face softened. She smiled and said, "Thank you for that!"

Anna turned from me, looked at the camera, and said, "Now I want to talk to my husband. Bill, I know you are watching this morning. I want you to go buy this book today!" She held up the book. "You take the test in the book. You're going to find out, like Dr. Sterling said, I'm an angel and you should do whatever it takes to keep me happy. Buddy, you had better have read this book before I come home today!"

The people on the set laughed and applauded.

She turned back to me. "I think your book will help many people."

I said, "Thank you! Now please call your husband after the show and tell him I'll buy him lunch today and I will give him my book."

Anna laughed and said, "I will. Thank you for coming in to talk to us!"

I said, "Thank you!"

The segment ended. Anna and I stood up as Susan walked out to us.

Anna said, "I didn't think I was going to like you. I thought you were a sexist pig with that stupid test, but you won me over. I believe you when you say you're trying to make men understand what they have in their wives."

I asked, "So is your husband going to be mad at me?"

"Are you kidding? My husband knows what he's got in me. He worships the ground I walk on. He knows he has a good deal. Plus, have you seen my husband?"

"No I have not."

"He's a hunk and rich. I have it good too!"

"You can't beat that," I said.

Anna said, "I'll call a few friends in New York. Ed, you're going to be in big demand. Susan, I want to thank you for bringing him to my attention. Sorry but I need to run now."

As we left the studio, Susan was ecstatic on how well the interview went. She said, "We have a blockbuster on our hands."

CHAPTER 18

AFTER THE LOS ANGELES INTERVIEW, television and radio producers across the country started to call Susan and set up interviews. Over the next week, I had several TV and radio interviews. All of them went well. I was starting to get comfortable talking to the media. The buzz about the book continued to grow.

I was to be the key speaker at a conference of magazine editors at a resort on Lake Erie, outside of Toledo, Ohio. Susan and I flew into Toledo. The resort was beautiful, right on the shore of Lake Erie. I enjoyed the time there. My talk with the editors went well. While we were there, Susan got a call from the producer of *The Horizon,* a popular nationally televised talk program that caters to women and is produced in New York. The show has four women hosts and a live audience. This would be a great forum to promote the book but Susan was concerned the interview was going to be unscripted. I told her not to worry; I could handle anything they threw at me.

On a Monday morning at 6:00, Susan booked a flight for us to New York out of Toledo with a connection in Cleveland. We got to the airport at the ungodly hour of 5:00 AM and went to the ticket counter. The ticket agent was a large woman with big hair that was an odd shade of red. She looked as if she was having a bad morning.

She said to us with a deadpan voice, no smile, and without a hint of being sorry, "There is a mechanical problem with the plane and it will not be repaired until this afternoon."

Susan said, "We have to get to New York today!"

The agent continued with the deadpan voice and said, "We have a bus and a limo to take passengers to Cleveland. It's a two-hour drive. Your flight is not until 10:00 so you will have plenty of time. The bus has left but the limo will be here in a few minutes for you."

I said, "That's fine with me."

The phone rang and the agent picked it up. I could tell from the conversation that the call was about our limo.

She finished the call and with no change in expression, she said, "Instead of a limo we have a cab for you. It's outside. The cab is prepaid including tip."

Susan said, "What happened to the limo? I would prefer a limo instead of a cab."

With some emotion, the agent said, "My idiot boss forgot to reserve the limo we always use. The limo is traveling to Detroit and will not be back in time. A cab is the only way to get to Cleveland in order to make your connection. It's waiting outside."

Susan asked, "Have you used this company before?"

"No, I haven't used them."

Susan turned to me. "I've had bad experiences in taxis. What do you think?"

"I'm sure we will be fine."

We walked out to the cab. At one time, it was yellow but now it was a drab, ugly tan. In the side and back windows, there were faded red window shades with small hanging balls on them. Loud Indian music was blaring from the radio. A young Indian man got out and opened the trunk. The driver was thin, in his early twenties with wavy black hair. He introduced himself in a heavy Indian accent and broken English. "I Arun. Where going?"

I said, "Cleveland airport."

"No been to Cleveland. Got directions?"

Susan blurted out, "Really? You don't know how to get to Cleveland? How long have you been driving a cab?"

"Week."

Susan cursed, "Oh crap! Let's talk to the agent, we need a different cab."

I said to Arun, "Wait here."

He smiled and said, "Okay."

We told the agent about the cab. She called the company and after a few minutes of heated discussion, we found out there were no other cabs available. We considered getting a rental car but the agencies weren't open. We had to use the cab we had. I had the agent write down detailed directions to the Cleveland airport. The drive on paper looked easy.

We go back out to the cab. Arun was asleep in the driver's seat. I walked to the driver's door and knocked on it, which startled him, and he woke up. He got out, rubbing his eyes, and walked to the curb with me.

I told him, "Okay, I have the directions. We take the toll road, which is across the street, and it takes us to Cleveland." I pointed across the street.

Arun looked across the parking lot to the street beyond. I could tell he was thinking about something. He asked, "Toll road needs money, yes?"

I said, "Yes."

"Have no money?" He reached into his pants pockets and pulled his pockets out. It must be a universal sign for no money.

Susan was frantic and asked the driver, "Really? You don't have any money. Ed, we are never going to get there!"

I said to her, "Calm down! It's an easy drive there; we will be on the road in a few minutes. We have plenty of time."

I turned to Arun. "Okay, I have cash and I will pay the toll. Can we go now?"

Arun smiled and said, "We go!"

We loaded the bags into the cab and got in. He started the cab, put it into drive, and took off like a drag racer. Our heads popped back from the acceleration. The toll road was across the street and I quickly had to yell at him to slow down and turn onto the toll road. I guided him there and we pulled up to the tollbooth with the tires screeching to a halt.

The tollgate was down and Arun only had to take the ticket from the toll machine for the gate to open. He was scratching his head on what to do.

He turned and asked, "Who lifts gate? You? Me?"

Susan yelled, "Take the ticket! Take the ticket!"

Arun looked at Susan. "Lady, why you mad?"

I patted Susan's hand to calm her down and said to her, "I got this."

I said calmly to Arun, "Please take the ticket and the gate will open."

Arun put down his window, reached out, and took the ticket. The gate opened. He turned and smiled at me then said, "American technology is wonderful! We go!"

Arun stomped the gas pedal and we zoomed out of the tollbooth. I guided him onto the toll road and finally we were driving east to Cleveland.

I said to Susan, "We will be fine now. It's a straight shot to Cleveland."

She said, "I need a drink."

We settled in for the ride but ten minutes later, I felt the car slowing down. I thought there must be something wrong with the vehicle. We pulled off to the side of the road and stopped.

Arun turned to us and said to me, "I tired. You drive."

Susan yelled, "No! No! No! You are the driver you have to drive. You are paid to drive!"

"I sleep now!" said Arun. He opened his door and got out.

Susan looked at me with eyes wide and said, "Don't you need a special license to drive this?"

"It's a car. I can drive it."

As I got out, Arun got in. Susan immediately opened the rear door on the passenger side and got out. We got in the front.

She said, "No way was I staying in the back with him!"

I looked at the dashboard and the controls. It looked like a regular car. Everything seemed normal; there was a half tank of gas and the yellow check engine light was on but it was running.

Susan said, “Can you drive it?”

“I think so,” I said.

“Should we go back to the Toledo airport?”

“I would rather get to Cleveland.”

I put the cab in drive and got back on the road. The cab had over 300,000 miles on it and shook when I went over sixty so I kept it at fifty-five. Cars and trucks flew past as if we were standing still.

A few minutes later, I looked back in the back seat and Arun was asleep. Soon, he was snoring loudly.

The rest of the drive was uneventful. I pulled up to the Cleveland airport and stopped. Arun was still asleep.

I asked, “What do we do with him?”

Susan said, “Leave him here!”

“He won’t know how to get back and he has no money.”

“That’s his problem!” She got out.

I opened the trunk and we got the bags out. I put the keys and $20 on the front seat so he could find them. We walked into the terminal. We went through security and Susan found a bar. It was supposed to be open only for breakfast but she bribed the manager for drinks. She had a Bloody Mary with breakfast and another one on the flight to New York.

I never heard anything more about Arun. I hope that he made it back to Toledo.

CHAPTER 19

WE ARRIVED IN NEW YORK that afternoon. I was scheduled to be on the Wednesday morning show. I turned on the television in my hotel room and promotions were already running about me being on the show. I was still getting used to seeing my face on television.

On Tuesday morning, we met with an associate producer and prepared for the segment. On Wednesday, we arrived at 8:00 AM for makeup and final prep.

My interview was with Ramona Thomas and Helen McDade. Ramona is an outspoken, smart, pretty, black woman who is never predictable in her opinions or questions. Helen McDade is a conservative, good-looking brunette who often asks probing questions. Susan was concerned because these two hosts had surgically dissected guests they didn't like in the past. From the prep questions they reviewed with us, I wasn't worried about the interview.

I was the third guest. In the audience were approximately 200 people, mostly women. The announcer said my name and the audience roared. As I walked onto the stage, people in the audience started throwing things at me. I was stunned at first and it took me a few seconds to figure out they were throwing different color panties at me. I couldn't tell if it was the sign of a protest or a sign of support. I was embarrassed when I sat down to the left of Ramona and Helen.

Helen smiled and asked me as the audience quieted down, "So, Dr. Sterling, do women always throw panties at you?"

I laughed and said, "No, this is a first for me."

The audience laughed.

Helen looked at the camera and said, "Dr. Sterling is the author of the book *Flannel Gowns and Granny Panties*. The book has been flying off the shelves and it has gotten great reviews. However, many women think the book is controversial, including Ramona."

Ramona said, "I've read your book. I do think it's controversial and I want to get right to the point. I wear granny panties!"

She stood, pulled up her blouse a bit, and tugged the waistband of her white panties up. The audience roared and threw more panties.

She looked at the audience and said with an attitude, "Dr. Sterling has an issue with granny panties and thinks women shouldn't wear them!"

The audience booed.

Ramona asked, "Dr. Sterling, let me ask you a question: Do you think I can't be sexy to my husband in granny panties?"

The audience was yelling in support of her.

I said, "Not at all, you're attractive and I'm sure your husband finds you sexy all the time."

Ramona said, "You got that right!"

The audience roared.

Ramona said, "I understood that when you counsel a couple you will tell a man he should leave his wife if she has a bad job, isn't pretty, and doesn't wear the right kind of panties! Am I right?"

The audience booed loudly.

Helen said, "Ramona, Dr. Sterling doesn't say that. In the book he says if a man has a good woman but for some reason the man doesn't recognize it then Dr. Sterling helps the man see how good she is."

"Thank you Helen, you're correct. Men often don't see what they have right in front of them. I try to make them understand what they have. Now, Ramona, let's say you and your husband hit a rough patch and you come to see me. I know a little about you. I know you're a mother and you enjoy cooking. You are attractive and intelligent. I would make sure your husband recognized all those positive qualities."

Ramona said, "You also got that right! My man would be leaving a perfect woman if he left me."

The audience applauded.

"Ramona, I agree with you. What I would tell you during the session is that granny panties are comfortable but aren't always sexy to a man. Would you agree?"

Ramona laughed, stood, and turned her bottom slightly to the camera. "Dr. Sterling, I look sexy in everything!"

The crowd roared. She sat back down. I laughed and said, "I agree, but could you be even sexier in something else?"

"Of course. In the right nightgown, I can make my man's heart melt!"

The crowd roared again.

I said, "That's the point I make in the book. A man usually responds to sexy underwear or a sexy nightgown. The right gown or underwear tells the man the woman cares enough to wear something special for him. Men aren't hard to figure out."

Ramona laughed and said, "You got that right too!"

The audience laughed.

Ramona asked, "So you never tell a man he should leave his wife?"

"Ramona, it's sad to say, but some couples aren't meant to be together. Let me tell you about one couple I counseled when I first started my practice. The woman had been married twice before. She was a three pack a day smoker, a heavy drinker with a bad attitude, and had a face and body that had seen many miles of bad road. She owned a business and was rich. The young man worked for her out of high school. He was a naïve young kid and he married the first woman he dated, which was this woman. Two years into the marriage, it wasn't working and she called me. What I saw in her was a mean woman who was trying to dominate the young man. She didn't want a husband or partner; she wanted a man who would cower to her. Once I knew them, I told the man there was no way the marriage could work because he was a strong young man. She didn't want that and she wasn't going to change. He soon realized I was right. They divorced; they each remarried and are happy now.

He found a nice girl and she found a young, sheepish guy whom she pushes around."

Ramona said, "I admire you for that. It seems like some counselors drag out the sessions for the money."

"I try to decide quickly if a couple can make it together. If they can, I want them to work it out by using my Sterling rules."

Helen looked at me and said, "I loved the Sterling rules. I especially liked the one where you say we have to let things go when a person says they are sorry."

She turned to the camera and said, "Dr. Sterling had a story in the book about a man who ran over his wife's cat. It was an accident and he said he was sorry. The woman loved the cat so much that she had it stuffed and put it on her dresser. The man had to see the dead cat every day. She often talked about the cat and about how much she missed it. On holidays and during the different seasons, she dressed the cat in different costumes. The cat never went away so the issue with the husband killing the cat never went away and it affected the relationship." She turned to me. "Please tell everyone how you helped the couple."

"I helped the woman to see that if she loved her husband she needed to let the cat go. With my help, she decided to bury the cat. They picked out another cat together and they are happy now."

Ramona said, "That's a great story."

I said, "I found myself in a similar situation. I once cracked an antique hand mirror my wife had gotten from her grandmother. She continued to use the broken mirror so I always saw it. It bothered me. However, I didn't talk to her about it and that was the issue. I finally did and she told me she wasn't keeping the mirror to punish me, rather that she kept it because she loved the mirror. We decided to have the mirror repaired. We did and the problem went away."

Helen inquired, "Dr. Sterling, what do you have against sweatpants? What do you call them?"

"Give up on life pants."

The audience laughed.

I said, "I see women going out with their men shopping or going to dinner wearing sweatpants. What the woman is saying to the man is, 'I have given up.' A woman's clothes don't have to be expensive but they should show you are a woman and that you're trying."

Ramona said, "Dr. Sterling, you're a brave man for coming here. You made me change my mind on you and your book. Thank you for coming!"

I said, "Thank you for having me!"

The audience started to applaud and threw more panties onto the set.

Afterward, Helen and Ramona hugged me. I gave them signed copies of the book.

Susan said, "You did a great job, I'm proud of you!"

"Thanks but if you don't mind, can we get a drink somewhere? I think a drink would help me unwind."

"You're asking me permission to have a drink? I had one for breakfast in order to be ready for the show. Let's go."

CHAPTER 20

IMMEDIATELY AFTER THE *HORIZON* SHOW, people started stopping me on the street, in airports, and in restaurants to discuss the book. I could tell many hadn't read the book and were simply telling me some other person's opinion but I enjoyed hearing people talk about it. The women seemed divided on the book but the men's responses were always positive. It was one of the best-selling books in the country.

I did two more interviews while I was in New York. After the last interview, I was tired. I had been on the road for a while and needed some time off. Susan and I took a cab to the airport. The flights were late because a bad storm had come through the New York area. Susan was going to Atlanta for a dinner and was agitated because the flights were late.

Susan tends to overpack when she travels. She had three large bags so we had to check them. The lines inside the terminal were long so we got in the line outside of the terminal on the curb. It was slow but at least it was moving. The longer we were there, the more agitated Susan got. We finally got to the front of the line and she immediately started to gripe at the skycap checking the bags. The skycap was a dignified older man with gray hair, probably in his late sixties.

Susan asked him in an angry voice, "Why are you the only person working this line? Three computer terminals are here but only one person working. Why is that?"

"The buses and subways are running behind due to the electric outages so some of our people are late getting here."

Susan got louder. "You mean there is not one person anywhere inside who can help?"

"Sorry, I'm the only one available."

"This airline's customer service is awful!"

"Ma'am, the bad weather is not the airline's fault."

"That's crap! The forecast said the weather was going to be bad today. The airline could have had extra people on hand."

The man was calm and didn't say anything. He took her bags and weighed them.

"Ma'am, I'm sorry but all your bags are overweight. There will be a twenty-five dollar overweight charge for each bag and a fifty-dollar charge for the extra bag."

Susan was so upset that the veins in her neck were bulging. She asked angrily, "What are you talking about? I didn't have to pay any extra charges on the trip out."

He smiled and said in a calm voice, "I'm sorry; it's the airline's rules, not mine."

"Okay, I will take them on the plane."

He smiled and said, "I'm sorry but these are oversized bags and will not fit in the overhead compartments. You will have to check them."

"This is ridiculous. I want to talk to your manager."

"Of course you can but he's working in the terminal somewhere. It may take thirty minutes or more for him to get here. Let me call him for you. Please stand over there and I will wait on these other folks till he gets here."

"I can't wait for thirty minutes! This is highway robbery!"

Susan took out her credit card and paid the fees. She threatened, "I will be sending a formal complaint to the airline about this."

The man finished and gave her the stubs. Susan stormed into the terminal. I was sure she was searching for a bar.

I was the next in line and said to the man, "I admire you for your patience. You were so calm and cool the entire time you were being yelled at."

"Was that woman with you?" he inquired.

I know the rule not to yell at service people who make or deliver your food or who can hurt you in some way. I responded with a lie, "No, she is not with me."

He smiled and confessed, "It was easy for me. You see, I could have waived the fees for the bags but she was being difficult. Whenever people are difficult, I follow the rules to the letter."

"I don't blame you. I would do the same thing."

He lowered his voice so only I could hear him. "There is one other thing. I shouldn't tell you this. She is going to Atlanta but one of her bags is going to Boston."

It took me a second to understand what he did then I laughed and replied, "Yeah, I don't blame you for that either."

He finished taking my bags and I paid him a large tip to make sure my bags would make it home. I started to walk away but my conscience got to me. I went back to the man.

I asked, "You know that lady who gave you the hard time?"

"Yes."

"Maybe she was just having a bad day and losing her bag could make a bad day even worse. Do you still have her bag?"

"Yes."

I asked, "Could I ask you to send it on to her destination?"

I handed him ten dollars.

"You're a nice man. You're right. You can keep the money. I'll make sure her bag gets to the right city."

I walked away and looked for Susan in the terminal but couldn't find her. Once I got through security, I got a call from my mother's cell phone, which was unusual. She hates using a cell phone so I knew it was something important.

"Hi Mom."

"Eddie, are you in town?"

"No, I'm in New York. I'll be home tonight. Is there something wrong?"

"Eddie, I need to talk to you about something important. Can we have breakfast tomorrow?"

"Sure, what is it you want to talk about?"

"I would rather we discuss it in person if you don't mind."

"Okay, how about having breakfast at 9:00 at Murphy's tomorrow?"

"That's fine, see you then."

When I arrived on Saturday morning, my mother was already there and she was talking to the matriarch of the Murphy family, Mrs. Kathleen Murphy. Mrs. Murphy is eighty-eight and is always impeccably dressed. She holds court at the restaurant every weekend morning, where she learns the latest gossip on everybody in Lake Forest and is always willing to share her advice on any issue. As I neared the table, they stopped talking, which was a clear sign they were talking about me.

Mrs. Murphy looked up at me and said, "There's the famous author, Dr. Eddie Sterling."

Mrs. Murphy expects a hug from people she likes. If she holds out her hand, it means she doesn't know you, doesn't like you, or has some issue to discuss with you. She doesn't hold out her hand so I gave her a good hug. If she kisses you on the cheek, you are in favor with her. I didn't get a kiss.

I said, "Mrs. Murphy, it's good to see you and it's good to see you too, Mom." I kissed my mother.

Mrs. Murphy said, "So I hear your book is doing well."

"Yes ma'am, it is."

Mrs. Murphy began the interrogation. "Why did you have to name it that awful name? I bet you didn't ask your mother about the title before you published it. Did you?"

My mother instantly replied, "No he did not! He didn't ask his father either!"

"Eddie, I thought you were a good boy and always talked to your parents about important things," said Mrs. Murphy in a disapproving tone while shaking her head.

"Mrs. Murphy, the title came out of the blue during the editing process. It's a long story!"

"It was still your responsibility not to embarrass your family; you should have spoken to your mother first!" Mrs. Murphy shook her finger at me as she talked.

I remembered at that moment that I had forgotten to call my parents about the book. I'm such an idiot at times.

"Mom, is the title of the book what you wanted to talk about?"

"I want to discuss the title and some other things. Mrs. Murphy, would you please excuse us? I think Eddie and I will have breakfast now and catch up on a few things. I'll stop and see you before I leave."

Mrs. Murphy said, "Please go ahead."

My mother got up and we went to another table. Once we ordered coffee and breakfast, Mother asked with emotion in her voice and tears in her eyes, "Eddie, why did you not tell us about the book?"

"Mom, I'm so sorry! I should have. Pam even reminded me to call you and I still forgot. I think I blocked it out because when I discussed the test in the book with Dad, he got upset with me. Dad and I argued about it at your anniversary dinner. I decided that it would be better not to talk to him about me writing a book."

She wiped tears from her eyes and said, "Well let me tell you how we found out about it. Your father and I were at the country club. Do you know Bill McIntosh?"

"Yes, he is a cardiologist and Dad hates him."

"He's the one that always says that Dad's not a real doctor."

"Yes, I have heard him say that."

"Anyway, we were at the club having lunch like we do every Sunday. Bill McIntosh came to our table and gave a pair of white panties to Dad. He asked Dad if he would have you autograph them. We looked at each other and we wondered why. Bill saw from our faces that we were clueless. He started laughing and said you had written a book. He went on and on in his loud voice about it. Everyone in the club could hear him. I'm sure he said granny panties ten times. I thought I was going to die!"

She wiped tears from her eyes then continued, "Two women visited after he left and said how much they enjoyed the book. They want you come to the club and talk over dinner. I can tell you now—your father and I will not be there! After the two women left, we quickly finished lunch and went to a bookstore. We bought two copies and read them that afternoon."

"Mom, I'm so sorry."

"Your father hasn't been back to the club since. He says we're canceling our membership!"

"He loves going to the club."

"Yes he does. He will get over it eventually. Did Pam know about the book?"

I decided not to tell the entire truth. I said, "Yes."

"Well thank God for that!"

I asked, "Should I call Dad and talk to him?"

"Not yet, your dad needs to think it through. I wanted to call you right away but he wanted me to wait. Don't tell him I talked to you. He'll call you when he's ready."

"Mom, you read the book. Except for the title what did you think?"

"Well, remember for the past forty years, I've heard about couple counseling and the strange things couples do and say. None of your stories surprised me. I hadn't heard your stories before but I have heard similar ones from your father."

"I guess you wouldn't have been surprised by my stories."

She seemed to perk up some and she said, "However, let me tell you something. The day after the panty incident at the club, I was at a doctor's office waiting in the reception room. Two women were there who had read the book. They talked on and on about how much they loved it. They said if a marriage counselor could save those crazy people in the book, if they needed a marriage counselor, they would come to you. Their comments made me feel good!"

I was pleased and said, "That's nice to hear!"

"I saw the interview you did in New York on *The Horizon.* I was so nervous but you did well. You were so handsome and articulate. I was proud of you!"

"Thanks Mom!"

"However, you should have also called me and told me you were going to be on TV!"

"I'm sorry; I should have talked to you."

"So you asked me if I liked the book. I went back and read the book a second time. I do like it. I hate the title and the stupid test but I like the book."

"How long do you think it will take for Dad to get over the book?"

She thought for a few seconds then said, "I don't know. It may take a while. He still hasn't accepted that new movies only come on DVD instead of VHS."

I laughed then replied, "Yeah, I know he doesn't like change. I had a hard time finding someone to transfer a DVD to VHS for his anniversary gift. The kid I used to do it thought I was crazy. He kept telling me people go VHS to DVD, not DVD to VHS. Eventually Dad is going to have to accept that the days of VHS movies are over."

"He will eventually."

I quipped, "Just in time for DVDs to become obsolete."

She laughed and said, "Yes, I know. I'm dreading that. Now switching to a happier topic, when do Pam and the girls come home?"

"They'll be home next week. I'll be out again for the book tour and will be back home the day after she gets back. I'm looking forward to the book tour ending and getting back to normal."

"I want things to get back to normal too. Now let's finish breakfast and you can tell me about what's going on with you."

We talked for an hour about the girls, my trip to Arizona, the book tour, and the people I met. I enjoyed being with her. I always do.

CHAPTER 21

On Sunday morning at 7:00, I got a call from my dad's cell phone. Dad believes he can call anytime. He gets up early and goes to bed late. I never get up early if I can help it, especially on Sundays. Dad gets along fine on five hours of sleep but my mother and I have always needed more.

"Hey Dad, is everything okay?" I said groggily.

"Everything is fine."

I looked at the clock in disbelief then said, "It's awfully early."

He said, "I've been up since 5:00. You should try getting up earlier; it will give you a new perspective on life."

"Let me make a note of that. Get up early on Sunday when I don't need to. Got it! Did you call to chat or do you need something?" I sat up in bed.

"I would like to meet with you."

"Pam and the girls are out in Arizona so we could meet for lunch today; I can stop by around noon." I was trying to get the meeting at home so my mother could be there to negotiate the peace settlement.

"I can't today. I haven't been to the club recently. Mother insisted we go today. She wants me to get out of the house."

I knew why he hadn't been there but I didn't say anything. I asked, "How about going to Murphy's later today for coffee?"

"No, Mrs. Murphy will be holding her royal court there and I don't want to see her. She asks too many questions. Can you come to my office sometime this week?"

I didn't want to go to his office, which is his turf. I wanted to meet him on a neutral field.

"Geez, Dad! I have a busy week. I'm trying to get caught up from traveling heavily lately, plus your office is across town from me."

He was adamant. "Eddie, I need to see you."

I knew I had to see him and I knew the rules. I had to call his assistant and make an appointment because he didn't keep his schedule. In addition, the appointment could only be before his office hours or after office hours unless there was an opening. It was the same way growing up. If I needed to see him during the day, I had to make an appointment.

"Okay, I will call Pat tomorrow and schedule a time."

"I'll see you soon."

The next morning, I called his assistant and luckily, there was an open slot at 9:00 on Tuesday.

On Tuesday, I showed up early. I brought scones and cappuccinos from a local coffee shop my dad likes. I believe it's always best to bring fresh meat to a lion because maybe the lion won't chew on you as much.

My dad's assistant is Pat Warfield who has been with him for thirty-five years. Pat and my dad are a good team and she is an excellent office manager. She is a large woman with short blond hair and is pleasant to work with. She is married with three grown girls. She will retire when my dad does, which could be twenty years from now. I have always liked her.

My dad's office is in a medical center. It's in the corner on the top floor and decorated with rich walnut paneling and oak furniture. The office is professional and stately. As a kid, when I entered, I always got quiet. The office had an imposing appearance to me. I opened the door and walked up to Pat's desk.

"Good morning Pat, am I still on for 9:00?"

Pat smiled warmly and said, "Good morning Dr. Sterling, yes he is running on time. He is doing some dictation now."

"I brought scones and cappuccinos."

"Thank you! Are they from Bennett's?"

"Yes."

"We love them from there."

"I know. I brought them as a peace offering. How mad is he at me?"

"Well when your book came out, he was upset. He had started to get over it but on Friday something came up and he needs to talk to you about it."

"There's something new? What is it?"

She said, "He should tell you."

"Okay, judging by your tone it must be bad."

Pat didn't say anything.

I asked, "Did you read the book?"

"Yes, I did," she said enthusiastically.

"Well?"

She giggled and said, "Don't tell your dad, but I loved it. I've been typing up your dad's notes for thirty-five years now. This is an emotional business and I've seen everything. I enjoyed your stories. You had a funny twist to them and I was pleased to see you have helped so many couples. I always said someone should write a book on the strange people who come to counseling and you did. I'm so proud of you!"

"Thank you!"

"There's one other thing I want to tell you."

I said, "Please don't tell me the type of panties you wear. I can't tell you the number of women who walk up to me now and show me their panties. I used to wonder what panties a woman wears but not anymore."

Pat laughed. "Don't worry; I'll keep that a secret. What I wanted to tell you was that your father and I watched the *Horizon* show together in his office. You did well! Your father thought so too. We were proud of you! I doubt he'll tell you."

"Thank you for telling me. Would you mind if I gave you a hug?"

"You haven't hugged me in years. I would love it."

I walked around her desk and gave her a big hug. My father opened the door and came out of his office as I was embracing her.

He said, "Pat, you should be careful with him! He'll probably want to check and see what kind of panties you're wearing."

Pat laughed. "I told him a few minutes ago that I don't wear panties. He seemed to like that."

My dad and I laughed. He said, "I've known you for thirty-five years and that's news to me!"

I said, "I never realized women can be so open on their choice of panties."

Pat said, "We aren't. I wanted to mess with your father."

My dad said, "Well, it worked."

We laughed.

Pat motioned to the treats. "Ed brought scones and cappuccinos for us."

My dad asked, "Are they from Bennett's?"

"Yes," I replied with pride.

He smiled. "Well I guess we should sample them."

My plan had worked. We each had a scone and a cappuccino. We chatted about one thing and another for ten minutes. My father seemed more relaxed.

"Son, thank you for the food, but we need to get started."

I walked inside and he closed the door. The office hadn't changed. Covering the walnut paneling behind his desk were his degrees and professional certificates. On another wall were his awards such as Counselor of the Year—and there were several of those. On another wall was what I referred to as the Eddie shrine. All of my accomplishments are on the shrine wall. He had pictures of me playing athletics from grade school to high school. He also had my college graduation announcements and the announcement of my practice opening. I was surprised to see a new shelf and on it was my book prominently displayed.

He sat behind his imposing desk and I sat in a chair across from him. He cleared his throat and said, "I know you talked to your mother about the book."

"Yes, we met for breakfast at Murphy's."

"I want to discuss two items with you. I will start with the book. I was surprised you didn't talk to me about it. The first time I hear about it is from my biggest detractor, Bill McIntosh. I would have rather had Satan tell me about the book than him."

"I'm sorry you found out from him."

"He dropped those panties on the table and for the life of me I had no idea why he did it. Why did you have to pick such an awful name?"

"The publisher thought it was catchy."

"You are a professional and you let some editor pick a name that embarrasses you, our profession, and your family?"

"Dad, wait a second. The book doesn't embarrass me. The book is well received and is doing well."

"You used lingerie to promote your book. You aren't embarrassed by that?"

"Dad, the world is full of people trying to get your attention to sell something. The title catches your attention but the content is what people like."

"You're proud of the content? The test is ridiculous!"

"Dad, the reaction that you're showing now is why I didn't talk to you about it. I knew you would blow up!"

"If you would have talked to me, I could have helped you from making this stupid mistake. I predicted what would happen if the Marriage Counselors Society learned about it and I was right. That's the second thing I wanted to talk to you about. The president of the society came to see me about you."

"What did he want?"

"Well, you know I was chairman of the certification committee for twenty years and conducted many disciplinary investigations."

"Yes."

"He came to me as a courtesy to tell me several members have written letters to the board with formal complaints about you."

I was upset. "Let me understand this. Several members have written letters to the board, which means my peers or competitors have complained, but none of my couples did."

"Yes."

I concluded, “They are simply jealous of the book’s success.”

“You need to take this seriously. If the society reprimands you, it could hurt your practice. I know of three times in the past when after the society reprimanded a member, the licensing board started an investigation.”

“Let them investigate. I did nothing wrong.”

“You’re being too cavalier about this. Any investigation can damage your practice. If the licensing board gets involved, you could lose your license and your practice.”

“I know you hold the society up as being something holy. I don’t. The society isn’t relevant any longer. They haven’t changed with the times. Many other counselors of my generation feel the same way. The International Marriage Counselor Group is the better organization. I’m a member of both. I bet I don’t hear a thing from the International Marriage Counselor Group because they don’t react to petty jealousies. If the licensing board contacts me, I’ll be open and honest with them. I know I haven’t violated any rules.”

“You swore an oath to never divulge any details of your couples’ discussions. Your book is full of private conversations you’ve had. Remember, I’ve reviewed your case files. I remember some of those couples.”

I fired back, “Name one.”

“Okay, the woman with the two husbands.”

“What about her?”

“I remember the case clearly. Her name was Kathleen Gregory. She was from Wisconsin. You didn’t change her name or where she lived.”

I countered, “I did change her name; her real name is Louise Meyer. They are actually from Illinois, not Wisconsin.”

“Are you sure?”

“Yes.”

He dismissed me. “Well, I remember it differently. You should check your files because I think you’re wrong and you used their real names.”

“Dad, I’m not wrong. I was careful about changing the stories and the people’s names to protect them.”

"I would never publish my couple's stories even if I did change their names."

"As you know, many men and women we counsel grew up as abused or neglected children. They grow up damaged, eventually marry, and find themselves in bad marriages with no ability on their own to improve the marriage or to change themselves. I believe when normal couples read the horrible stories of couples who worked through their problems then maybe they will be encouraged to work on their marriages. You have to admit; we have helped some damaged people in the past."

"Yes, I agree."

"In the book, only two couples got a divorce. I wanted people to know that marriages can be saved," I said.

"That's good to know."

"Dad, I came here to apologize for not telling you about the book because I should have. I'm not ashamed of the book. I worked hard on it and people like it. People have told me they are using my rules to improve their relationships. I know you don't agree with the test and we have a different opinion on it. So I'm sorry I didn't tell you about the book and you found out the way you did."

He sat there for a few seconds then said, "I accept your apology. Anyone else could have brought the book up to me and I would not have been as upset but Bill McIntosh is a real ass. Between you and me, Bill is on his third marriage. He told me that he and his wife were having trouble. He asked me if I would be willing to provide counseling for them. I didn't take him on as a client."

I smiled and said, "Now look who's being selective in taking clients."

"Yes, I have been more selective. When we talked I thought what you said about being more selective was a good idea."

"So why didn't you take Bill as a client?"

"I've decided that anyone whom I counsel must be willing to listen and be able to change. I think Bill is a stubborn ass who will not listen to me. Each of Bill's wives is younger than the last one. This one was barely twenty when they married. A forty-year difference in a couple is hard to deal with."

"I agree. So Dad, are we good?"

"Yes, but I need you to do one thing for me."

"Sure. What do you need?"

"Can you sign Bill's damn panties? He sent me a pair and he calls me every day to ask about them. He wants to frame them for his office."

I laughed and said, "Sure, do you want me to send him a signed copy of the book?"

"No! If he wants a signed book, let him buy a copy and send it to you."

"That's fine with me."

My father opened his desk drawer and removed a package. He handed it to me.

I opened it and looked at the panties. "This is a large pair, is his wife a large woman?"

"No, she's probably a size two."

"I wonder who owned these."

"I asked him and he said they were his mother-in-law's."

"No kidding? His wife is going to let her husband frame a pair of her mother's panties in his office. I could see a good story coming from this in the future."

I signed the panties and placed them back in the package.

"Thank you for signing the panties and for coming to see me."

"You're welcome. I'm sorry for everything that happened."

"That's all behind us now."

We hugged then I left after kissing Pat goodbye. As I drove to my office, I was glad that I came to see him. I remembered having the same feelings when I was kid. I always made the visits to see him at the office to be something that I dreaded but in reality, every meeting with him there always made me feel better.

CHAPTER 22

I HURRIED TO MY OFFICE and when I arrived, Sally brought two registered letters to my attention. The first letter was from the society requesting a meeting later in the week on complaints they had received.

The other letter was from the licensing board. One of my clients had contacted the board and filed a complaint. The licensing board requested a meeting to discuss it. Of the two letters, this one was the most important and very upsetting.

The rest of the day, I had normal meetings with clients. None of them asked any questions about the book. That evening I went home to an empty house because Pam and the girls were still in Arizona. I was feeling lonely and I saw Ricky was home.

I went to see him. I rang the front doorbell and he answered the door in gym shorts and a sleeveless T-shirt with *Marines* written on the front. This was his normal at home attire.

He said, "Well if it's not the famous author. Come on in."

I stepped in and Brenda was there; she gave me a hug. We walked to the family room and sat down. They sat on a couch and I sat in a recliner.

She said, "It's good to see you. It has been a long time since we've seen you and Pam."

I said, "It's good to see you too. I'm not so sure that I can say the same about the Marine."

"I know. You have to take him in small amounts."

Ricky said, "That's because I'm such a radiant personality. Speaking of being radiant, we saw you on TV."

"How did I do?"

Ricky said, "TV puts on ten pounds for most people but for you it was more like twenty. I thought you looked like a porker. You need to work out more."

Brenda said, "Ed, ignore him, I thought you looked handsome! He's mad because he put on his dress uniform this morning and it doesn't fit anymore."

"That's because I've put on more muscle across my chest," Ricky said proudly as he stood and flexed his muscles.

Brenda reached over, patted his stomach, and said, "I'm sure you added something but I'm not sure it was muscle."

Ricky flexed his muscles again. "I'm in great shape."

"Calm down, big boy, I was only teasing." She tugged at his arm; he sat down then she kissed him on the cheek.

"On the *Horizon* show, they must have thrown a hundred pair of panties at you. Did you get to keep any of them?" inquired Ricky.

"No, I was too embarrassed."

"I would have."

Brenda said firmly, "Over my dead body!"

Ricky said, "Sure I would have, they're like trophies."

Brenda asked, "So do you have women's panties as trophies?"

"Dear, I only have yours!"

"Good answer!" said Brenda.

Ricky asked, "So are women asking you to sign their panties?"

"Yes, it happens all the time now," I said.

"So do they pull their pants down in front of you or what?" Ricky asked.

"I've had several women ask if I would sign their panties. I said yes then they leave and return later with panties. I don't know if they go to the bathroom and remove them or what."

Brenda exclaimed, "Oh that's gross!"

Ricky said, "Not to me."

Brenda smacked him on the arm. "Okay, no more discussion about panties!"

Ricky asked, "Did Pam see you on the TV shows?"

"I don't think so. Her dad's place in Arizona is remote; there's no Internet and they have bad TV reception."

"You should be grateful that she didn't see you. I bet she wouldn't have been happy about the panties being thrown at you," said Ricky.

Brenda said, "I said no more panty discussion!"

"Okay, switching topics, when is your father-in-law going to return my lawnmower?" inquired Ricky.

Brenda asked, "What are you talking about?"

Ricky replied, "Your uncle stole my lawn mower."

I said, "No he didn't."

"That's how I remember it," Ricky said.

I asked, "Brenda, do you remember when your lawnmower burned?"

"Oh yes, I remember it well. I came home from shopping and it was by the curb still smoking. It was an expensive mower and he couldn't get it started. He took it back to the mower dealer several times. It would start at the dealer but not at home."

I said, "It wouldn't start because he kept flooding it."

Ricky said, "No, it was a defective mower."

I divulged gleefully, "The Marine poured gas on it and torched it."

"You lied to me. You told me it caught on fire," Brenda said in an upset tone.

"It did catch on fire. I just provided the match." Ricky smirked.

"You burned it? Why would you do a stupid thing like that?" she asked.

I butted in and said, "I was home when he did it. I saw the smoke billowing up from the backyard. I ran over with a fire extinguisher and he was standing near it watching it burn. He said he torched it because it wouldn't start and he was fed up with it. I put out the fire then he pushed it to the curb. My father-in-law came over later that day and saw it. He asked me if he could have it. I said Ricky was throwing it away so sure he could have it. He took it home and repaired it. He never had one issue with it. It starts with one pull. He's had it for years now."

"I pushed it out to the curb because it was still smoking not because I was throwing it out. I was going to repair it," Ricky said with conviction.

Brenda blurted out, "You hire an electrician to change a light bulb. You were never going to repair that mower!"

Ricky was now defensive. "I was going to try. Anyway, in my opinion, your uncle stole it."

Brenda frowned, stared at him, and shook her head. She said, "I'll talk to you later about the lawnmower. Let's change the subject. Tell me, how is Aunt Flora?"

"She's doing better and Pam should be home soon."

Brenda said, "That's good. So how's the book doing?"

"The book is selling well but it has caused some problems for me at work."

I told them about the society and the licensing board complaints.

Ricky said defiantly, "Screw them! If you don't think you did anything wrong, then stand your ground! They'll back off. Remember the Federal Aviation Authority investigated me right after 9/11. After those planes hit the towers and the Pentagon, every flight near Washington was under scrutiny. I had a flight there and they accused me of violating the restricted airspace. I flew lower than the minimum to avoid a civilian plane that was in my path. It took weeks to verify that I did the right thing. You have to be aggressive or the bureaucrats will run over you."

"I feel the same way."

"You let me know if you need a Marine to show up. I look impressive in my dress uniform."

Brenda, in a teasing tone, said, "The Marine will have to get his uniform altered first due to his muscle growth."

Brenda and I laughed. Ricky did not.

I said, "I'll let you know if I need the Marines."

We had a few beers and I left late. It felt good to be with friends again.

CHAPTER 23

On Thursday morning at 9:00, I had a meeting with the Marriage Counselors Society in downtown Chicago. I hate going there. I had worked there each summer during college and graduate school when my father was on the certification committee. I always felt when I entered the society's offices I was going back in time at least thirty years. Everything seemed old. The decorating, the office furniture, their methods and the people, all of it seemed old and out of touch.

I was prepared for the meeting. I had brushed up on the bylaws and recent legal activity that had occurred with the society. I was to meet with the president, Dr. Marc Collins, and Dr. Mary Beetle. The receptionist took me to the boardroom.

I didn't know Dr. Beetle, but I knew Dr. Collins well and I don't like him. I worked for him when I was there. Dr. Collins was in his late sixties. He was fat, bald, and wearing a wrinkled gray suit with a red tie that was too short for his large belly. His white shirt was too small in the neck and looked like it was choking him. Dr. Beetle was in her early fifties. She was tall and thin with long black hair pulled into a ponytail. She was wearing a black suit and black high heels. She looked like Olive Oyl from the Popeye cartoons. They were standing at a credenza getting coffee when I arrived.

As they made their coffee, I remembered when I worked there. Every day at 10:00, I brought Dr. Collins coffee from a shop around the corner from the office. It was a special Turkish coffee. He always had it with three creams and two sugars. Not once in six summers of working there did he ever thank me for bringing him the coffee and many days he didn't pay me for it. The last summer I worked there, I started to change the coffee I brought him. I would get a different brand or decaffeinated coffee then I would add extra cream or sugar or some flavoring. He asked about it but I didn't admit anything. On my last day there, I thought about adding a laxative but at the last minute, I lost my nerve and didn't do it.

Dr. Collins was lazy, an arrogant ass, and a terrible manager. I was afraid of him then. I thought he and the society were a powerful force in my industry. I know better now.

Dr. Beetle said without looking at me in a high-pitched, grating voice, "Take a seat."

I already hated her whiney tone.

I sat down. They finished making their coffee then sat down. I was irritated they didn't offer me any. I didn't want it but since they didn't offer, I wanted some. I got up, went to the credenza, and poured a cup. The coffee had a strong aroma like the Turkish coffee I used to get. I took my time putting the cream in. I went back and sat down.

Dr. Beetle, in an even higher voice, said, "I hope you're comfortable now!"

Sarcastically, I said, "I'm cozy, thank you." I sipped the coffee, although I thought it tasted like paint stripper.

I asked, "Dr. Collins, is this your special Turkish blend?"

"Yes, it is. I see you're a connoisseur of fine coffee."

"Yes, I am. I remember when I used to get this for you every day from the shop around the corner."

"I don't remember that."

I wanted to say *Of course you don't, you old, fat snob!* I bit my tongue and smiled.

Dr. Beetle said, "Today's meeting is to determine if we should convene a full disciplinary panel to examine the complaints brought against you. If we determine there is any validity to the complaints, then we will schedule a panel meeting. Do you understand?"

"I think so."

"There are three complaints."

"From whom?"

"We don't have to tell you who filed the complaints."

"Let me make sure I understand. I can't know my accusers?"

"No you cannot! We want to be able to protect the members."

"I see. Can you tell me what the complaints are?"

"I can summarize them for you."

"I can't read them?"

She said, "No, you cannot! Before we go too far, I will not say the name of the book because it's embarrassing to me. So I will say, 'Your book.'"

I decided to be an ass so I asked, "So you are embarrassed to say flannel gowns?"

"No."

"Are you embarrassed to say panties?"

"Yes, in mixed company I am."

"Do you wear panties?" I put extra emphasis on the word *panties.*

"That is none of your business."

I said, "I will take your answer as you don't wear panties."

She quickly replied, "Of course I wear panties."

"Do you wear granny panties?"

Indignant, she said, "Again, that is also none of your business. Dr. Sterling, you must take this meeting seriously."

"I do take this seriously. Do you have more than three pets?"

Dr. Beetle leaned back in her chair and said, "Now I see. You're asking me questions from your test. You're trying to evaluate me."

I smirked because that was exactly what I was doing. I asked, "I have one last question: Are you a practicing counselor?"

"I was, but I work at the society now full time for the certification committee as an investigator."

"How long have you worked here?"

"Two months."

"Is this your first investigation?"

"Why is that pertinent?"

I said, "I was wondering how much experience you have."

"This is my first investigation. Now getting back to the subject at hand, regarding your book. One of our members filed a complaint that your book was not peer reviewed. Our bylaws state any publication by one of our members must be peer reviewed. This is a serious problem! What is your response to the complaint?"

I replied, "My book is not a study and doesn't challenge any current counseling methods or procedures. It doesn't have to be peer reviewed."

She asserted proudly, "The bylaws say any publication must be peer reviewed."

"Dr. Beetle, I worked here for several summers and I worked for the certification committee. I still keep track of all bylaw changes. In 2007, the society disciplined a member for not doing a peer review when he published a book called *Spicing up Your Marriage*. The member sued and won a large judgment. The certification committee, after losing the lawsuit, amended the bylaws to allow books without peer review under certain circumstances. This book clearly falls under those guidelines. This organization never throws anything away. I'm sure you can find the files on it."

Dr. Beetle looked at Dr. Collins and asked, "Is he right?"

He replied, "I remember the lawsuit now. Yes, he is correct."

Flustered, she said, "The other two complaints deal with the test in the book. Who developed the test?"

"I did."

"On what approved counseling procedures was this test based?"

"None."

She smirked and said, "Dr. Collins, he said none. This is a serious violation!"

I asked, "Why?"

"We cannot have counselors using untested methods to determine which clients or couples they counsel."

"Why?"

"Because it is unethical."

"Why?"

She protested, "Dr. Sterling, you're being difficult!"

"No, I'm not. Where in our bylaws does it say I have to counsel every couple?"

"It doesn't, but it's an ethical issue. You are using a sexist test to determine the couples you select."

"Let me think about this for a second. Were the two people who complained about the test women?"

She was surprised then stammered, "I cannot tell you that."

"I can tell by your response that they were women. Did they say my test was sexist?"

"Yes they did. In their opinion and mine, the test is sexist and shouldn't be used."

"My test allows me to select the couples I counsel. Our bylaws say I can run my business any way I want as long as I follow accepted counseling techniques."

"Our women members are offended by the test in the book."

"Tell them not to read the book."

She said, "It's not that simple."

I said, "Why not? It is a commercial book, not a psychology journal. Some members may be offended but there are no rules saying I cannot use a test, sexist or not."

"We are trying to establish a new precedent here."

"Maybe instead of trying to punish me, why not change the bylaws? All the members can then vote on the change."

She said, "We have to demonstrate to our members that we are aggressive in protecting the image of the society."

"Going back to my history here again, the society has done what you're doing with me in the past and lost again in court."

She asked, "What are you talking about?"

I said, "The society reprimanded a member who refused to counsel a couple after the husband was verbally abusive to the counselor when he discovered the counselor was Jewish. The couple had worked with the counselor for a year and had invested considerable money in fees. The counselor felt he could no longer give the couple unbiased advice. The society's position was that the counselor had to continue the counseling. The counselor sued and the society lost when the court ruled for the counselor. This falls in the same category—I can choose whomever I want to counsel as long as I follow our rules for not being discriminatory."

Dr. Beetle looked at me for a second then turned to Dr. Collins. "You haven't said a damn thing! You were the one who wanted to pursue this because your girlfriend was one of the members who complained. Do you have anything to say?"

Dr. Collins cleared his throat and said, "Dr. Sterling, we will take your comments into consideration. At this point, I'm leaning toward having the full certification panel review these complaints. It will require you to answer questions in front of the full panel. We will send a letter to you with our decision on what the next steps will be."

I said, "I knew you wouldn't listen but I tried. I know you'll stack the certification panel to rubber stamp whatever you want accomplished but let me tell you this clearly: You will lose in court if you reprimand me. In the two cases we discussed, you lost large judgments that were over a million dollars each. I will sue you for much more and I will win."

Dr. Beetle said, "We can outspend you and drown you in legal bills."

Anger flared up inside me and I said with a loud voice, "I used to work here and I know how you operate. Look around here—you don't have a spare penny to spend to spruce this dungeon up. You will not risk money on a case that you will lose. I'm not afraid of you and I have the money to fight back. I look forward to talking to the panel then counting my money later when I win the lawsuit if I am reprimanded."

I got up and left the boardroom. I had defended myself and it felt good. The complaints against me were groundless. I hoped my aggressive stance would keep them from moving ahead.

CHAPTER 24

THE NEXT MORNING WAS THE meeting with the licensing board; I knew I would have to take a different tactic with them. It's a government agency so I needed to answer their questions carefully.

The licensing board offices are in downtown Chicago. The licensing board must not have much political pull because it's not in the modern Government Center office building but in an old rundown brick building down the street. The offices are on the fifth floor.

A security guard led me to a conference room. He had to be over seventy and walked slowly. He hummed a tune as we walked; he acted as if he had no worries in the world and wasn't in a hurry.

I asked, "You seem to enjoy your job."

"This is the best job I have ever had. All I do is walk people back and forth to rooms. No one bothers me and I get paid a good state salary with a pension."

"How long have you been doing this?"

"I've been here since I retired as a detective, which was twenty years ago."

"Wow, how much longer do you expect to work?"

"Till I'm old and can't walk anymore. I'll have two state pensions when I retire."

"Good for you!"

"Have you been here before?"

"No."

"I take it you haven't met the lady you're meeting with."

"No."

He divulged, "She's a little strange."

"What do you mean strange?"

"You'll see. She also feels she can ignore the rules."

"How does she ignore the rules?" I asked.

"She thinks I don't know she smokes in the conference room but I know she does. She's taken over the conference room so she can secretly smoke."

He opened the door and stepped in. A woman was sitting at the end of a long table. The guard was right about her—she was unique looking with her short, black, spiked hair and painted-on eyebrows. She was pale, thin, wearing black lipstick, a black mini-skirt, and a black blouse. I would have never thought she was an investigator for the licensing board; she looked more like a member of a rock band.

The guard looked at the woman and said, "This is Dr. Sterling."

He sniffed the air and asked, "Has someone been smoking in here?"

The woman replied, "Not that I know of."

The guard looked at me, winked, and said in a whisper, "She's lying." He left.

The room was hot and the window was open. You could hear the city traffic noises. She had been smoking in the room. There was no question about it; the stench was still in the air. I saw a pack of cigarettes and a lighter next to her black bag. A large pile of manila folders was stacked in front of her.

She said, "Have a seat. My name is Kandy Johnson. That's Kandy with a K. I'm an investigator for the licensing board. We don't investigate every complaint but you are a well-known person. My boss thought we should look into this one so no one would think we ignore complaints about famous people."

"Lucky me," I said sarcastically.

"By the way, I've read your book."

I thought this couldn't be good. "You did?"

"Yes, my boyfriend made me read it and we took the test."

I stayed quiet; I wasn't sure what to say.

"Do you want to know how I did on the test?" she inquired.

"I bet you scored high," I lied. I hoped flattery would help me in this situation. "You're attractive and I can tell you have a good job."

She smiled and said, "Thank you for the compliment! I did score high, near the top of the scale. I'm fun to be with, I'm an excellent cook, I have no pets, and I wear sexy underwear at all times."

I said, "I'm not surprised." I then stopped and corrected myself. "I mean, I'm not surprised about the score, not about your underwear."

"No worries; I knew what you meant. My boyfriend and I are having some trouble. Would you mind if I talk to you about it?"

I thought, *Why not listen to her story? I'm stuck here anyway and maybe she will be lenient on me if I help her out.* I said, "Please go ahead."

She stood up, took her pack of cigarettes and lighter, then walked to the open window. To the right of the window on the wall was a large, no smoking sign. She took a cigarette, lit it, then took a long drag. She blew the smoke out of the window then leaned on the wall, next to the sign.

"My boyfriend and I have been together for two years now. He's an attorney in a large law firm downtown here. He's older than I am. I'm thirty-five and he's fifty-five. We met at a club. He said he was attracted to me because I was different. I love rock music and I like to party. At first, he adored everything about me. Now he wants me to change. He wants me to change my hair, my clothes and he wants us to stay home more. He wants to buy a home in the suburbs. Do you see my problem?"

I thought, *Oh yes, I see the problem. This is a couple that I would have a difficult time saving.* I said, "Yes, I do. I have seen this before."

"So give me the quick version. Do I dump him or play along to get his money? He's loaded. I could act as if I'm going to change, marry him, then divorce him then take half his money. I can always go back to the way I am now after I have his money because I like who I am."

"Do you love him?"

She raised her painted eyebrows. "You're the second person to ask me that."

"Who else did?"

"My mother. My friends say marry him then take his money."

"It's important you love him, don't you think?"

She said in a matter-of-fact way, "I like being with him. I like the security and the money. He's smart and kind."

"I haven't heard you say that you love him."

"Yeah, I know."

"I think if you marry him you should love him."

"Yeah, my mother said the same thing."

"Your mother sounds like a smart lady."

"Yes, she is."

"You said your boyfriend is an attorney, right?"

"Yes."

"Has he talked to you about a prenuptial agreement?"

She looked dismayed then said, "Yes. He mentioned it recently but I'm trying to get him to drop the idea."

"He's an attorney. He won't."

She pondered for a few seconds then stated, "Maybe my boyfriend and I should see you."

"I would enjoy that."

She sat down at the table and said, "However, there's a little issue we need to resolve first. Let's discuss the complaint. We received a complaint from a Margaret Thornton."

"Who is Margaret Thornton?"

"Margaret Thornton is eighty-two years old and lives in Chicago. Her son is a prominent politician in Cook County, which is another reason why this complaint is on the fast track."

"What is her husband's name?"

"Cory."

"How old is Cory?"

"He's fifty-eight."

"How long have they been married?"

She thumbed through the papers and answered, "Three years."

"I don't know the couple."

She asked skeptically, "Are you sure?"

"Yes."

"She said they came to you but you wouldn't help them. She later heard you talk about the book on the radio. She believes you probably used the test in the book and decided not to help them. She believes that you concluded she wasn't worth having as a spouse. She feels she was discriminated against because of her age. Her husband left her, filed for divorce and now she lives alone. How do you feel about this?"

"I think it's incredibly sad. When did she say she came to see me?"

"Ten months ago."

"I'm sorry but I don't remember them."

Her tone got dark and accusatory. She said, "Dr. Sterling, this complaint is damning! Why did you decide not to help them?"

"Ms. Johnson, I can't answer your question because I don't remember her."

"This is a serious problem."

"I understand, but I don't know the couple."

"Dr. Sterling, you should remember that lying to an investigator can result in the loss of your license."

"I understand."

"I need your permission to examine your case files, your billing records, and your schedule. Do I have your permission?"

"Absolutely!"

"I will call your office and set up a time. I have nothing else for today. Thank you for coming in!"

I left the office. I was worried about the meeting because I didn't remember Mrs. Thornton. She may have stopped in and I quickly talked to her. My memory for people that I have only met once isn't great. I also don't always keep records on couples whom I don't counsel. I remembered thinking that this could end up being my word against Mrs. Thornton's. I felt I was in serious trouble.

CHAPTER 25

My mother-in-law's health had improved and Pam came home after having been gone for eight weeks. She had missed the TV interviews and the publicity campaign. I called her daily to tell her what was happening with the book but with her parents' home being in a remote area, she didn't understand how much press coverage there was.

I was finishing a swing through the southern states doing TV interviews in Atlanta and Charlotte. I would be home three days after Pam arrived home. Several neighbors stopped in to talk to Pam about the book. Pam told me she was surprised at how positive people were about it.

Lisa Bronson is a popular Chicago TV personality who normally deals with soft news and gossip stories. Her forte is catching celebrities and politicians in embarrassing situations by using hidden cameras. Lisa is in her early forties, attractive, has long, curly, red hair and always wears expensive, fashionable clothes with flashy jewelry. She is divorced, terribly nosey and she moved two doors down from Ricky a few months back. Brenda had met her but didn't know her well. Once my book came out, she started to visit and text Brenda often. She eventually asked Brenda if she could introduce her to Pam.

Pam visited with Brenda on the day she got home. Lisa showed up uninvited. Brenda introduced her and Lisa asked Pam if she could interview me. Pam said she would ask me but she didn't think it would be a problem.

I learned later that Pam was wearing sweatpants on the day she met Lisa. Lisa must have thought filming the wife of the author of *Flannel*

Gowns and Granny Panties with his view on sweatpants would be a funny piece to run on air. Over the next few days, Lisa had a hidden camera crew follow Pam. The crews videoed Pam in pajamas and sweatpants at the bank, the pharmacy, and at the grocery store.

When I got home from the southern trip, Pam asked me to call Lisa. I called her and we agreed to an interview, which we did at our home. Nothing special happened during the interview. Lisa's questions I had answered many times before. Pam was also included in the interview, which was new for her, but she did well.

After the interview, Lisa told me she knew Susan. I was surprised she knew her. She asked me several questions about Susan. Since she was a gossip reporter, I gave her generic answers. She asked about Susan's engagement and I avoided the question entirely.

The weekend after the interview, Pam and I went to dinner in downtown Chicago. When we entered the restaurant, the hostess recognized me. She was a pretty woman in her mid-twenties. She said, "Dr. Sterling, I loved your book."

I replied, "Thank you!" I glanced at Pam, who had a surprised look on her face.

"Could I get your autograph before you leave?" asked the hostess.

"Of course."

"When I saw your reservation, I was hoping you were the author. I set aside our best table for you."

"That was nice, thank you!" I said.

She took us to our table and we sat down.

Pam said, "Well aren't you the famous one? Does this happen to you often? Because if it does, I'll start hanging out with you more!"

"It happens more than I would like it to. I was at a McDonald's recently and a woman asked me to sign a napkin."

The waiter came to the table. "Dr. Sterling, it's a pleasure to have you with us. The owner is sending a complimentary bottle of champagne to the table. He loves your book and wants your autograph. He will be over in a few minutes."

"Thank you!"

"I will be right back with the champagne."

As he left, Pam said, "Geez, I'm impressed and embarrassed. I seem to be the only one in Chicago who hasn't read your book. I'm sorry I didn't read it. I should have been more involved."

"The past few months have been busy for us. It was tax season and then your mom got sick. You can read it now."

"I'm looking forward to it."

The waiter and a man came to the table. The man was tall with blond hair, a square face, and a big smile.

The man said in a booming voice with a Swedish accent, "I'm Gustave Johansson, I'm the owner. Thank you for coming to my restaurant! This is a special French champagne, I'm sure you will enjoy it."

I said, "Thank you! You're so kind. If I could have your address, I will send you a signed copy of the book."

"Thank you, but if you don't mind, I sent my assistant to a department store to get two pairs of panties. I have heard you have signed them for other people. I would like to hang a pair in the restaurant and another pair in my office."

I laughed and said, "It happens often. I would be happy to."

Mr. Johansson opened the bottle and poured two glasses. He said, "Please enjoy!"

After he left, Pam said, "Oh my god! This is unbelievable! A few weeks ago, my husband was an unknown, nice man who helped people in their marriages. Now he is a rock star who is recognized by everyone and signs panties."

I smiled and said, "I hope you'll start treating me better since I'm so famous."

She smiled, patted my hand, and said, "Poor baby! You have it so rough."

"Yes, I do."

Pam said, "So do people have you sign panties often?"

"Oh yes! It's embarrassing at times. My dad had me sign a pair for a guy at the club."

"Your dad! You're kidding me!"

"No, it's true."

Pam said, "Any woman who whips off a pair and asks, 'Please sign this' will have to answer to me."

"Several times women have asked me to sign panties then came back quickly with them in hand. I wondered where they came from!"

"I won't wonder; I'll tell the woman to take off." She laughed and said, "Sorry, I mean shove off!"

I laughed as well.

A few minutes later the hostess came to the table and had me sign the panties. I also signed a book for her. They took pictures of us. Several people stopped at our table and asked for autographs. The dinner was outstanding and I enjoyed the time with Pam. It was the last peaceful period I had before all hell broke loose.

CHAPTER 26

On Monday, I left for a two-day trip to promote the book at a trade show in New York. That evening on the six o'clock news, the interview with Pam and me aired. The piece had the interview with the two of us but also showed Pam running around town in pajamas and sweatpants. Lisa said according to the test in the book, Pam would get points off for how she dressed. Lisa suggested Pam would also get more points off if she wore the wrong kind of panties. She included a clip from *The Horizon* where women were throwing panties at me. She suggested in a grocery tabloid way that Pam should worry since other women were throwing their panties at me.

The segment was intended to be a humorous piece, and to most people it was, but not to Pam. She was embarrassed and shocked about the segment.

As a partner in a prestigious worldwide accounting firm and on the fast track to become a managing partner, Pam is conservative, private, and always concerned about her professional image. The video showed her in pajamas, in sweatpants, and with no makeup. Pam later told me that her phone blew up from the texts and phone calls from people at her office after the segment aired.

I was at a dinner when she texted me in all capital letters, *OUR TV INTERVIEW WAS ON TONIGHT. IT WAS AWFUL AND EMBARRASSING!*

I texted, *Why was it bad? I thought it went well!*

Lisa had a crew follow me and filmed me in sweatpants and pajamas doing errands. I looked awful.

I texted, *You don't look bad in anything.*

Did women throw panties at you on a show in New York?

I had not told Pam the details of the *Horizon* interview. I texted, *Yes.*

Lisa said on the segment that I should be worried about losing you! Should I be worried?

I was appalled that Lisa would say that sort of rubbish about me. I texted, *No, she is just being sensational to grab viewers. We can talk about it when I get home.*

When do you get home?

I texted, *I will be home day after tomorrow. I should be home by 5:00.*

Okay, she texted.

I texted, *I love you. I will see you day after tomorrow.*

She didn't reply. I knew she was upset.

Susan was with me at the dinner and she received texts about the interview. After dinner, we watched the video on her tablet in the lobby of the hotel. Susan was livid and told me I couldn't have any more interviews unless she approved it. As it turned out, Lisa and Susan hated each other.

That evening, a national TV gossip show picked up the story and talked it up. They included the footage of Pam around town in sweatpants and pajamas. To make matters worse, a late night comedian joked about us during his monologue.

Pam had missed the TV shows from the night before but learned about them from her friends the next morning. She got angrier. She got the book from my home office and read it. As Ricky predicted, she went ballistic. She also looked up the *Horizon* interview on the Internet. She was shocked at the women throwing panties at me.

As I have said before, Pam has a fiery temper and when she is upset, everyone knows. Pam went to see Brenda and two of our neighbors were there. Everyone heard firsthand from Pam how upset she was. Ricky was on a trip. He texted me about what he heard from Brenda and it was bad. Ricky said I was in deep trouble with Pam. I tried to call Pam but she didn't pick up.

Someone told Lisa that Pam was upset about the book and the *Horizon* interview. Lisa knew Pam always locked me out when she got upset. She thought it would be a great follow-up story to video it. She set up a camera crew in a van in her driveway to capture the event.

I got home from the trip expecting the worst. I pulled up in the driveway and the garage door wouldn't open, which I had expected. I walked to the back door but it was locked. I walked to the front door and rang the bell. Pam answered the door wearing sweatpants.

I said, "Hi honey, I have been trying to call you."

She yelled, "I'm so mad at you about this damn book! You have embarrassed me in front of my friends, clients and my bosses!"

"How did I embarrass you?"

"You didn't tell me you were writing the book about me!"

"The book isn't about you."

"The hell it isn't! I took the test. I get points off because I wear sweatpants with a logo on the butt. I get points off because I wear camo and pajamas outside in public. I also use the bathroom when you are in it and I have three pets. I'm a terrible cook, I hate to clean, and I don't like any of your sports. What else do I do wrong? Oh yeah, I wear flannel gowns and granny panties!"

She turned and pulled her sweatpants down, showing her panties.

After she pulled them back up, she yelled, "I didn't know you were judging me!"

"I haven't judged you!"

"Yes, you have! That damn test is all about me! I failed it and everybody knows!"

Pam slammed the door. I stood there. I rang the bell but she didn't answer. After a couple of minutes, I walked back to the car. I drove to a hotel nearby and checked in. I tried calling her but she didn't answer.

I didn't sleep at all that night. I went to work the next morning and had a miserable day. At the hotel the next night, I watched the early local news. In a promo, there was a video of Lisa asking the audience to stay tuned for her segment on the evening news at 6:00 because she had a juicy update on the *Flannel Gowns and Granny Panties* author. My cell phone rang. It was Susan.

She said without a hello, "I told you not to do any more interviews unless I approved it! Did you do another interview with that nosey redhead?"

I said vehemently, "No!"

"I saw a promo that she had a juicy update about you."

"I saw it too. I don't know what it is."

"Did Pam do an interview?"

"I don't think so."

"Ask her."

"I'm not home."

"Call her."

"I can't right now."

"Why not? This is important!"

I confessed to her, "Pam kicked me out of the house last night. I'm in a hotel and she won't take my calls."

"What did you do wrong?"

"She's upset about the interview with Lisa."

"I see. Let's talk after the segment airs."

I was nervous waiting for the segment to run. After the real news was over, Lisa appeared.

She said, "Recently, I had an interview with the nationally known author Dr. Ed Sterling. Dr. Sterling is a prominent marriage counselor who practices here in Chicago. In my first segment last week, I showed Dr. Sterling's wife running around Lake Forest in her pajamas and sweatpants, which is bad according to Dr. Sterling's famous marriage counseling book. Well, ladies and gentlemen, apparently Dr. Sterling is in hot water with his wife over the book. From what my sources have told me, she was out of town for a long period caring for her sick mother and didn't know about the book. She wasn't aware that her husband thinks flannel gowns, granny panties, and sweatpants are a bad thing for a marriage. Apparently, Mrs. Sterling wears all of these. The following video catches Dr. Sterling on the front steps of his home with his irate wife. She sends him packing and now Dr. Sterling is living in a hotel."

The video showed everything that happened at home and even included me checking into the hotel. At the end, it showed several times in a video loop Pam turning and showing her pink granny panties. I was shocked and knew I was now in deeper trouble with Pam.

Lisa said at the end of the segment, "As you can see, Dr. Sterling is in trouble at home. I understand Dr. Sterling's father is also a marriage counselor. Dr. Sterling, maybe you should give your dad a call."

My cell phone rang and it was Susan.

She said, "That wasn't too bad. It was actually kind of funny."

I screamed at her, "Funny! This isn't funny! My wife is going to kill me!"

"Ed, calm down! It's not that bad."

"I can't calm down. They showed her bottom on TV."

"You couldn't see her bottom. It was pixelated over."

I replied, "Yes but you can still tell."

"Don't worry, this will actually increase the book's sales."

"Susan, I don't care about the book. My wife is berserk over this!"

"She'll get over it."

"You don't know my wife. This will affect her at work."

"She will be fine. People forget these things fast. This'll blow over by the weekend."

"She may file divorce papers by then."

"Don't be overly dramatic. Hold on a second, I'm getting a call."

She was gone for a minute then returned.

She said, "Do you have your tablet with you?"

"Yes, why?"

"The video of you and your wife has gone viral."

I said, "Oh god no!" I hung up. I searched the Internet and found the video. It was the same video but Pam's bottom wasn't pixelated now. You could clearly see her granny panties. Now I was starting to get text messages from my mother, Dad, then Pam.

I checked Pam's first. In all caps she texted, *DID YOU SEE MY BOTTOM ON TV?*

I was trying to lighten the drama of the moment so I texted, *Yes, I thought you had a nice bottom.*

She replied in all caps, *DON'T GET CUTE WITH ME! THE FIRST INTERVIEW WAS BAD BUT THIS ONE IS WORSE!*

I didn't think it was so bad, I texted back.

Everyone in Chicago knows that I wear granny panties and that you are staying at a hotel!

Pam, this will blow over. People will laugh about it then forget it.

I won't. My bosses won't. My clients won't. I'm the laughingstock of the accounting world. I should resign now.

I texted, *This kind of thing will be hot for a day or two then it will blow over.*

Again, in all caps, she texted, *I GOT A TEXT FROM A FRIEND AT WORK. THE VIDEO IS NOW ON THE INTERNET! I AM LOOKING FOR IT.*

A few minutes passed and Pam texted back.

In all caps, she texted, *NOW EVERYONE IN THE WORLD CAN NOW SEE MY BOTTOM CLEARLY! I AM GOING TO DIE!*

I replied, *Pam, let's get together and talk about this.*

NO! I DO NOT WANT TO SEE YOU OR TALK TO YOU. YOU STAY IN THAT CRAPPY HOTEL AND THINK ABOUT WHAT YOU HAVE DONE TO THE GIRLS AND ME!

I texted her to try to get her to reconsider but she didn't respond. As you would expect, the text messages from my parents weren't happy either.

The night got worse. A national TV gossip show and the late night comedy shows played the video. Pam's bottom was seen clearly everywhere. People who hadn't talked to me in years were calling and sending me texts. Everyone thought it was hilarious.

I had a miserable night with no sleep. The next morning, I went to the office. News and media people were waiting outside my office, wanting interviews. I had to plow my way through a crowd to get to my office door. I told them I couldn't talk then but I would answer their questions later. I had Sally call building security to have the media moved to the lobby. I closed my door and then I called Susan.

I begged her, "Susan, I need help! This has gotten out of hand. I couldn't get into my office because there were so many media people here. I had to call security to get them moved."

"No kidding! How many were there?"

"Twenty or so."

"Wow that's great!"

"What do you mean great?"

"All this publicity is great for the book. I have never had this kind of buzz before."

I pleaded with her, "Susan, please listen to me! My life is falling apart! My wife won't talk to me! I'm being investigated and I'm living at a hotel!"

She said, "Calm down, this will blow over!"

I screamed, "I'm not going to calm down! You don't understand what this is doing to me. Pam means everything to me! She is my Bobby; I can't stand being without her!"

The phone was quiet for few seconds then she said, "I'm sorry. I get it now. I was only thinking of the book and myself. Come here tonight and we will work on a plan."

"I will."

"Don't talk to anyone!"

"I won't."

CHAPTER 27

CARLA MET ME OUTSIDE SUSAN'S office. She hugged me and said, "I'm so sorry all this stuff is happening to you. You're such a nice man; you don't deserve this. Are you doing okay?"

"No I'm not! The world seems against me at this moment."

"I know. Susan will figure out a plan to deal with it."

We entered Susan's office and she hugged me.

"Please have a seat. Would you like something to drink?"

"Yes, I need Jack Daniels and lots of it."

"No problem, we have it. Carla, could you bring us some?"

"Sure, I would be happy to."

Carla left and we sat down.

"So tell me everything. I need to know all the details."

I talked about what was happening. I told her I felt as if my life was crashing and I didn't know what do to about it. I told her about the licensing board and the society investigating me. I told her that I have never felt things were so dark for me. I had a hard time seeing how I could straighten all this out. Carla came back with the drinks then left. We drank some of the whiskey.

Susan said, "Let me show you something."

She walked over to a pile of folders on top of a filing cabinet and pulled out a purple file. She came back and sat next to me. She opened the file and took out a yellowed newspaper article then handed it to me.

The article's heading was *Prominent editor has breakdown at work* and it included a picture of the police leading Susan from a building.

She said, "Please read it."

I took a couple minutes to read it and I looked at her after finishing it.

"Did you see who the reporter was?" she asked.

I read the by-line and it was Lisa.

She said, "I had a breakdown a few months after Bobby died. I was simply overwhelmed. I got under my desk and I wouldn't come out. Someone called the police and there was a terrible scene. The publishing company I was working for at that time eventually fired me. It was a bad time in my life. Did you know anything about this?"

"No."

"This should show you that time helps take care of things. When I lost Bobby, I didn't go to see anyone for counseling, and I should have. Things got out of hand and I had the breakdown. I was in my early twenties when I started to experience things I couldn't explain. My mother committed suicide when I was eight. My father would never talk about her illness so I didn't know I had a hereditary mental disease. Bobby was the first person to tell me that there were two Susans."

"So you know about the two Susans?"

"Yes, I know there is a good Susan and a bad Susan. Without medication, I can't really control which Susan you see. When I'm taking the medication, people see the good Susan. However, the good Susan is not a good editor. The bad Susan is the award-winning editor. She can see a book clearly. I know the bad Susan is difficult to work with and no one can live with her. Eventually each of my fiancés discovered my problem. They start to ask questions and I end the engagement before I get hurt. Bobby had started to see it. He wanted to discuss it but he died before we could. I was willing to give up being an editor and take the medication to be his wife but then he had his accident."

"Susan, I'm so sorry."

"There is nothing for you to be sorry about. If I carefully watch myself, I function well. As part of my treatment, I garden and have learned to cook. I also meditate and I do yoga. When I'm home, I have to keep busy with something other than publishing work. I have always wanted to cook but as you know, I cannot focus for long periods. I need to walk away when I start feeling the stresses. When I'm cooking if I walk away at the wrong time, my cooking comes out bad."

"Do you taste your food?"

"No, I don't want to be disappointed but people seem to like it because my food always goes quickly."

I smiled and didn't say anything. I asked, "Does medication help?"

"Yes, but the meds don't allow me to work well as an editor. I can manage the symptoms usually without the meds. I went away for a few weeks, as you know. I left because I felt a bad episode coming. I took my meds while I was gone. After I came back, things were fine for a while but I didn't feel on top of my game so I stopped taking them. I know I got a little wild on our trip to Las Vegas."

"Yes, you did."

"I'm sorry if I embarrassed you. I don't remember much about it except for that big woman who sat next to you. She kept putting her hand in your lap for some reason. You need to tell me the story of what happened because I don't remember much and my mind keeps telling me you have a thing for big women."

I laughed and said, "I don't have a thing for big women and there is a funny story about you and the big woman. Someday I will tell you."

She said, "I want to apologize to you about something else. I knew how women would react to the test in the book. I sent a copy of the book to a testing company. They have people read our books and they gauge the reactions. The report on the book was the most polarized I have ever gotten. Women absolutely hated the test. The testing company recommended removing it. The book was rated high without the test but I wanted a reaction because reactions sell books. I'm sorry I didn't tell you about the testing we did. I knew better."

"It's not a problem. My best friend, who read the book, told me the same thing. He recommended removing the test; I should have listened to him," I replied.

"Now this issue with Pam—do you think you can patch it up?" asked Susan.

"I'm trying to talk to her but she's angry. My wife is a lovely woman but she has a hot temper like her mother. She has gotten mad at me in the past over minor things and locked me out for a few minutes. She has never locked me out for this long. I know a couple shouldn't go this long without talking. I'll keep trying."

"I have an idea on how to fix this but I'm working out the details. You'll have to trust me for a while. Now the key thing is for you not to do any interviews or have any discussions with the media until the plan is completed."

"What do I do about the media? I know I was followed here."

"They can only hurt you if you talk to them."

I said, "They will continue to follow me and probably video me at the hotel."

"You staying at the hotel is old news. Just ignore them for now."

"I also have another problem. There have been complaints filed against me with the licensing board and the Marriage Counselors Society."

"Do you know why yet?"

"Yes, I've met with them and I'll be having some additional conversations with them this week."

"Are the meetings open to the public or to the press?"

"No."

"Do they publish minutes of your meetings?"

"No."

"I know what can happen if you lose your license, but what happens if the society says you did something wrong?" she asked.

"I can lose my certification, which will hurt my reputation. You don't want to lose it but if you do you can still stay in business."

"Have there been any complaints to the licensing board or to the society before?"

"No."

"That's good; I trust that you will deal with those two items. I will gear up the publicity machine once I've worked out the details of my plan. Now there's good news. The book sales are fantastic. We are the number-one bestseller in electronic books and print. I know it's not consoling to you but it's a good thing."

"Well I'm glad at least the book is doing well."

Susan said, "I promise you, it will get better. You'll be back with Pam soon."

We finished the drinks and she hugged me. I left the meeting feeling better. I had someone on my side.

CHAPTER 28

KANDY, THE LICENSING INVESTIGATOR, CAME to my office, interviewed Sally, and went through my files. As I suspected, I didn't have anything on Mrs. Thornton. I prayed I hadn't been negligent in my paperwork.

Kandy scheduled another meeting for me at the licensing board. I arrived on time and sat in the waiting room. I was there only for a couple of minutes when the old security guard arrived and took me to the meeting. He wasn't happy like he was the last time I saw him.

He asked as we walked, "Have you seen Kandy recently?"

"No."

"You're in for a surprise."

"A good surprise?"

"I think so, but maybe you won't."

"Is she still breaking the rules?" I asked.

"Yes, but I don't care anymore."

"How come?"

"There have been some budget cuts. They're retiring me so I don't care if she burns the building down."

"Is retiring a bad thing?"

"Yes; I don't want to stay home with my wife. She's hard to live with."

We stopped in the hall outside of a conference room and he looked both ways to see if anyone was coming. The hall was empty, and he asked quietly, "You're that marriage counselor guy, right?"

"Yes."

"Maybe we should come see you. I don't know why my wife is always so upset with me but she always is."

"Have you asked her why she's so upset?"

"Oh no, I don't talk to her. I'm afraid of her."

"You were a cop, right?" I asked.

"Yes, but even cops get scared."

"I see. I'm sure I can help you. Please give my office a call and schedule an appointment." I handed him a card.

He read it, put it in his shirt pocket then said, "We'll see you soon. Now Kandy wants you to just take a seat in the room and listen. There's someone else with her."

"Okay."

He opened the door and we walked in. Kandy was sitting at a conference table next to an older woman. I almost didn't recognize Kandy because she had changed so much. Her black hair was a short, cute style and she was wearing normal makeup and conservative clothes. I sat down at the table across from the older woman who I suspected to be Mrs. Thornton. Kandy ignored me.

Kandy asked her, "Mrs. Thornton, thank you for reviewing the details of your complaint. I have a few more questions for you. Did you pay anything for the meeting with Dr. Sterling?"

"Yes, I did."

"Do you have the canceled check?"

"I paid in cash."

"Do you have a receipt?"

"Somewhere but I couldn't find it."

"You are sure that you paid for a session."

"Absolutely. The woman there gave me a receipt."

Kandy asked, "Mrs. Thornton, do you remember what Dr. Sterling looked like?"

"Oh yes, I remember him well. He is a handsome gentleman."

"Mrs. Thornton, is Dr. Sterling about the age of Ed here?"

Mrs. Thornton looked at me, smiled, and said, "No, Dr. Sterling is much older."

Kandy asked, "Are you sure he's older?"

Mrs. Thornton smiled and said, "Oh yes, I'm sure."

"Mrs. Thornton, thank you for coming in today. Once the investigation is completed, I will contact you."

"Thank you for listening to an old woman and her troubles." Mrs. Thornton got up slowly and walked to the door. Kandy got up and opened it for her.

Mrs. Thornton left and Kandy closed the door. She walked over and sat on the table next to me. She smiled and said, "Well, my investigation is over. You saw that Mrs. Thornton had no clue as to who you are."

I was relieved and said, "Yes, thank goodness!"

"After looking at your files and meeting with your assistant, I felt something was wrong. Mrs. Thornton described to me a completely different person when we spoke over the phone. I believe she looked up Dr. Sterling in the telephone book and she didn't know there were two Dr. Sterlings. The other Dr. Sterling met with her and decided not to counsel her."

"Did you know the other Dr. Sterling is my father?"

Kandy laughed and said, "I did not. It's a small world."

"He is Edward James Sterling. I am Edward Steven Sterling. In the phone book, he comes first. Did you talk to my dad?"

"I talked to his assistant, Pat. Mrs. Thornton and her husband met with your dad and for whatever reason he decided not to counsel her."

"So is this investigation over?"

"Yes, I wanted you here so she could see you so that I could confirm everything."

"Well thank you for being so diligent about this."

"You're welcome."

"I notice you're looking a little different."

"Yes, I am. What do you think?"

"Well I thought you were pretty before but I like this new look."

"So does my boyfriend and my mom."

"Why the change?"

She said, "I thought about what you and my mom said. I want to give the relationship a chance. I thought there could be a few things that I could change."

"Well, I wish you luck. Relationships are never done; you always have to work on them."

"Yes, that is rule three in your book."

"Exactly. Well, thank you again."

She picked up a cigarette.

I looked at her and shook my head.

She said, "I know. I'm not supposed to smoke here."

"You shouldn't smoke at all."

"My boyfriend and my mom say I shouldn't smoke and now you."

"We're all right."

"I know, but there are only so many things I can work on at one time."

"I understand."

I left feeling as if a major storm had passed. I was not out of trouble yet because I still had the society to deal with but at least my license was no longer in jeopardy. I went back to the hotel and soon the good feeling from the day drained away. The sadness of being alone again in a drab hotel took its place.

CHAPTER 29

A DAY AFTER THE LICENSE board meeting, I got a registered letter requesting I attend a formal certification hearing at the society's offices. Like before, the letter didn't specify the complaints or my accusers. I immediately called and set up the meeting for the next morning. I went to the hearing prepared and ready to do battle.

I arrived on time and a secretary escorted me to the society's boardroom. I immediately saw I was going to have an uphill battle because Dr. Beetle had stacked the deck against me. Six women were there with her plus Dr. Collins, sitting around one end of the table.

Dr. Beetle sat at the end of the table opposite from me. She started the meeting and said, "Dr. Sterling, we are here to discuss the complaint filed against you. This is a certification hearing. If this panel finds you have violated the bylaws of the organization, you could be reprimanded. Do you understand?"

I replied, "I do. I thought there was more than one complaint."

"There is only one. The complaint is that you have used the private conversations of your clients to publish a book. The conversations of our clients cannot be relayed to anyone and especially for the enrichment of the counselor," said Dr. Beetle.

I looked around the room. Several of the women were nodding their heads in agreement.

I said, "I have some questions for you."

"Dr. Sterling, we aren't going to conduct this session like the last one. You were rude to Dr. Collins and to me. We will ask the questions this time, not you," said Dr. Beetle.

I said aggressively, "That is crap and you know it! I defended myself against three complaints, which were untrue. I didn't let you push me around that day and I will not today either."

Dr. Beetle said, "Dr. Sterling, you must remain professional!"

"I will be if you are. Now in our last meeting you said there were three complaints. What happened to those?" I demanded.

"We determined those complaints had no merit," said Dr. Collins.

I exclaimed, "Well thanks for telling me! Did you ever think I might want to know?"

Dr. Collins said, "We expected to tell you today."

Sarcastically I said, "I bet. I should have known of the new complaint before I got here."

Dr. Beetle said, "We don't have to review the complaints with you prior to this meeting. Our rules say complaints are presented at the panel hearing."

"Why did you bring me in to discuss the other complaints?" I asked.

Dr. Beetle said smugly, "It was a courtesy to you but your bad attitude last time caused us not to extend the same courtesy this time."

"I see. Since I took you to school last time on the rules and proved you were wrong, you wanted to surprise me this time."

She smiled and said, "No, we are simply following the rules. You seem to know the rules well."

I said, "I do know the rules and I have an issue I would like to discuss about this hearing."

She asked, "What is it?"

"I don't think this panel reflects the demographics of our membership. I count seven women and one man. This panel doesn't seem balanced to me."

"I will make note of your objection but I don't agree," said Dr. Beetle.

I asked, "Dr. Beetle, you chose the panel, didn't you?"

"Yes."

"Seven women and one man seems fair to you?"

"It does. I picked who I thought was best for this complaint regardless of their sex."

"Really? I find that hard to believe."

"I have noted your issue. Now let's move on," said Dr. Beetle.

I asked, "This new complaint was filed after our last meeting?"

"Yes."

I was suspicious so I asked, "Did anyone here file a complaint?"

"We don't have to tell you," Dr. Beetle replied.

"So someone here can be my accuser and my judge."

"Yes."

"That doesn't seem fair to me. Ladies, do you feel having my accuser here is fair?"

One woman said, "I don't."

Another one said, "I don't either."

I said, "I think whoever filed the complaint should be excused from this hearing. They shouldn't judge me."

Dr. Beetle confessed, "I filed the complaint. In my opinion it was an obvious violation of our ethics."

I asked, "Does anyone else see a problem with her being on the panel?"

Several people nodded yes.

I demanded, "You must excuse yourself from this investigation."

"I will not."

I stood up, leaned over the table, pointed at Dr. Beetle, and repeated my demand. "You must excuse yourself from this investigation!"

Several side conversations started. Dr. Collins looked around the room and had a worried expression. He said, "Dr. Beetle, I will take over for you."

Dr. Beetle said angrily, "No, I can handle this."

Dr. Collins insisted, "Please wait outside."

She got up and left.

Dr. Collins growled, "Are you happy now?"

I smiled at him, sat down, and said, "Yes, let's proceed."

Dr. Collins said, "The complaint states that you cannot use your patients' information in a commercial book."

"Why not?" I asked.

"The discussion between a patient and a counselor is private and confidential," said Dr. Collins.

"I agree, but I protected the couples' identities. No one knows their names or where they live."

"That's not enough," said Dr. Collins.

"In our business, don't we often publish the stories of our clients in professional journals?" I asked.

He replied, "Yes but your book is not a professional journal. It is a commercial piece. You're making money off your couples' troubles."

"I know my book has helped people. People have told me so. Also, not one client has complained. The only people who have complained are my competitors from my trade group," I said.

"Sometimes we have to speak on the behalf of our clients," said Dr. Collins.

"I agree if we conduct harmful practices or do clearly unethical things, but the use of the stories helps others. Every client I counsel signs a waiver that allows me to use their stories. I also called everyone and got their permission in writing again before I published the book. No one turned me down."

Another counselor asked, "Your clients sign waivers?"

"Yes, according to the International Marriage Counselor Group, we should have couples sign waivers as a standard practice. They believe using the stories—without the names, hometowns, and details of the private conversation—can help other people. I agree with them."

Another counselor said, "If the clients signed waivers, why am I wasting my time on this? We have a full time investigator who should have looked into this matter in more depth. Dr. Collins, you convinced us that having a full time investigator would improve the quality of our organization. If this investigation is an example of how we will use an investigator, then I don't think we should have one."

"I agree," said several others. The panel was talking among themselves and one woman was clearly upset.

Dr. Collins said, "I will take your comments under consideration. Dr. Sterling, I believe I speak for the panel when I say that once we verify the waivers you described, this complaint has been resolved." He stood up, walked toward me with his arm out to shake hands. I stood up and for an instant, I almost didn't shake it but my father's face flashed through my mind so I did.

Once the panel investigation was over, the tone in the room changed. The panel members crowded around me and asked about the book. I watched Dr. Collins open the door and talk to Dr. Beetle, who was sitting outside. I don't know what the conversation was but it was animated. They were gesturing and pointing at each other. Neither of them returned to the boardroom.

It was late Friday and since I wasn't living at home, I was in no hurry. Several from the panel went with me to a bar across the street and had drinks. Dr. Beetle was the subject of the conversation. The women didn't like her and I made sure they knew the details of our last meeting. I left that night believing Dr. Beetle would soon need to start looking for a new job.

CHAPTER 30

I WAS AT THE HOTEL over the weekend and I was miserable. I stayed in my room, had room service, and watched TV. I wanted to stay out of sight. I felt alone and I missed my family. I was anxious to hear from Susan but so far, I had heard nothing. I was beginning to believe she couldn't help me. I called and texted Pam but she didn't respond.

I went to work on Monday and it was a normal day. After work, I was driving to the hotel when I got a text from Pam.

Please watch channel seven tonight at 6:00.

I texted back, *What?*

It's important; watch channel seven.

I rushed to the hotel and turned on the TV. Fifteen minutes into the broadcast, a reporter came on. She said, "I have the pleasure of talking to Mrs. Ed Sterling, the wife of Dr. Sterling, the famous author of *Flannel Gowns and Granny Panties.* Mrs. Sterling, welcome."

Pam was in a TV studio with the reporter and they were sitting on two tall stools. On a screen behind them was a picture of my book. She was beautiful. I missed her so.

Pam said, "Thank you for talking to me."

"I understand you have pulled off one of the best publicity stunts I have ever seen. Lisa Bronson, who is a reporter on another network here in Chicago, reported that you and your husband were at odds over his book and you had kicked him out. She had this awful video of you and your husband getting into a fight. I understand none of it is true."

"You're correct, none of it is true. We staged it. When Lisa asked for the first interview, I suspected she had an agenda in mind. I soon saw a camera crew tailing me. The camera crew was definitely not very good at undercover work. They were driving a white van and whenever I stopped three guys with a camera would pour out of it like circus clowns. I guessed what they were doing. I couldn't reach my husband, who was out of town, so I called his editor, Susan Fairchild. Together we dreamed up the publicity stunt."

"So you wore things according to your husband's book that a woman should never wear."

"Well, the first day they followed me, I was wearing sweatpants because I had gone running that morning. After that, we thought I should ham it up a bit. So I wore sweatpants, pajamas, and other things out in the public."

"Now the video of you showing your bottom and kicking your husband out was hilarious."

"I did go a little over the top showing my bottom but I thought it would get people's attention."

"It did. The video was one of the most popular so far this year on the Internet. You really pulled the wool over the eyes of Lisa Bronson, didn't you?"

"Yes, we did. Lisa is always so nosey and loves gossip. It was easy to get her excited about this."

"I have to give it to your husband, he's a good actor."

"Well to be honest, I didn't tell him about it because he can't keep a secret. When I kicked him out on the video, he didn't know yet about the public relations stunt."

"So you booted him out and he didn't know it was a stunt?"

"Correct, I told him later that day. I apologized to him. He's a good sport and laughed about it."

"So let me ask you: Do you wear granny panties?"

"I do at times. They are comfortable but I also know when not to wear them." Pam looked at the camera and winked.

The reporter laughed and said, "I understand what you mean. Your stunt worked—the book is more popular than ever. Have you considered going into acting or public relations?"

"No, I'm happy being an accountant—but now I need to tell my husband something, if that is okay?"

"Please go ahead!"

Pam looked at the camera and said, "You can come home now. The stunt is over."

The reporter said, "Well, congratulations to everyone. I love this."

I stood there in shock.

Five minutes after the segment ended my phone buzzed. It was a text from Pam.

Eddie, please come home. A smiley face was at the end of the text.

I texted, *I will be there soon.*

I was elated. I immediately packed up and headed home as fast as possible. I drove up to the garage and pushed the garage door button. I waited but it didn't go up. I sat and asked myself, *Did Pam really text me?* I checked my phone and she had. I pushed the garage door button again but it didn't move. I wondered what was going to happen. I walked to the front door and all the neighbors were on their front steps watching me. Lisa was also on her front steps with her hands on her hips watching. I rang the bell.

I heard someone struggling to open the door then Gracie opened it.

I smiled and said, "Hi monkey, may I come in?"

She smiled and said, "Yes Daddy, we not mad no more."

She opened the door and let me in. Natalie and Pam were there. Gracie hugged me and so did Natalie. I kissed the girls then kissed and hugged Pam. The dog was barking and the parrots were talking in the background. It felt good to be home.

I said to Pam, "I've missed you."

Pam said, "I've missed you too."

I said, "I'm so sorry for everything."

"Me too."

"I have many questions about what happened today. I'm really out of the loop."

Pam said, "We can talk about that later."

I said, "We should close the front door in case there's a camera crew watching."

Pam said, "I hope there is! I may start answering the door in my underwear."

I closed the door to be safe.

The rest of the evening, we caught up. Pam had managed to keep the kids kept away from the media buzz so they didn't know any details other than that Pam had been mad at me. The kids told me about their Arizona trip and everything they had done after I left. Gracie was still excited about our adventure on the backside of the mountain. She whispered to me that she still wanted to pee outside again someday.

I had gotten presents for Pam and the girls in the various places I had visited on the book tour. We had a good time opening the gifts and talking about where they were from. Soon, I was feeling at home again. We put the girls to bed and then came back downstairs. I opened a bottle of wine and we sat on the couch.

I said, "I'm confused about today. Did you really do what you said on TV? Was there a publicity stunt?"

Pam answered, "No. I got a call from Susan. She said she had an idea on how we could clear up the mess we were in. We met at her office. She wanted to keep you out of the loop on the plan. I know it was a little cruel but we wanted you to still act like you were down and out."

"Boy, I was never so down in my life. My wife kicked me out *and* I was in trouble with the society and the licensing board. It was a bad time for me!"

"I wanted to ask you about that, is it all cleared up?"

"Yes it is, thank god!"

"That's great to hear."

I said, "Tell me more about getting together with Susan and the stunt."

"You might know this, but there is a bad history between Lisa and Susan. They worked together years ago. Lisa was always into gossip and she wrote the article about Susan when she got sick."

"I saw the article."

"Lisa could have killed the story but she decided to publish it. Susan hates Lisa for that and for a few other things over the years. Susan dreamed up the story of a publicity stunt. With her connections in the media, it was easy to set up. All I had to do was play my part on the interview. You will be interested in this: The woman who did my interview hates Lisa more than all of us combined."

"Wow! Aren't you and Susan afraid this story will get out?"

"Not at all! Only you, Susan, and I know the details. Susan said in a few weeks no one will care except Lisa."

"Has the publicity caused you a problem at work?"

"I thought it would but it hasn't. Not one client asked me about it. My bosses think it's funny. A new prospect actually asked my boss if I could submit a proposal for her business. The prospect is a woman and she told my boss that she's worn sweatpants and granny panties from time to time as well. Also my staff bought me a pair of pink granny panties, framed them, and hung them on the wall."

"I'm so glad to hear you weren't affected."

"No I wasn't, but I let my temper control me again. I'm sorry."

"You don't have to be sorry. I caused all of this."

Pam said, "Maybe I should consider going to an anger management class."

"Or maybe your husband should learn to stop pissing you off so much."

She laughed and said, "Let's put it behind us because you and I are back together and that's all I care about."

"I agree."

Pam kissed me passionately. "I missed you terribly!"

"I missed you too."

She smiled and said, "I made reservations for us to get away for a few days. I talked to Sally and she has freed up your calendar. We're going to have a long romantic weekend."

"That's wonderful!"

I kissed her.

Pam said, "Also because of the book I will be packing a little differently for the trip."

"You will?"

"Yes, I won't be bringing my flannel gown or sweatpants but you will have to learn to accept my granny panties."

I said, "I don't care what kind of panties you wear. It is okay with me if you don't wear any."

She smiled and said, "For a large part of our romantic weekend, I promise I won't be."

Without providing any details, I can tell you that we had a great time!

EPILOGUE

TWO YEARS HAVE GONE BY. Susan is still at the publishing company but Carla is taking a leave to have her first child. She married a year ago. Pam and I went to the wedding. It was beautiful.

Susan started seeing a different therapist who convinced her to try a new medication. She is doing great and the bad Susan is gone most of the time now. There is news about a new boyfriend—or rather, an old boyfriend. Mike and Susan are dating and have gone into couple's therapy to try to see if they can learn to live together. Susan asked if I would be their counselor but I got my dad involved because I felt I was too close to them. According to Dad, they are making excellent progress. He expects an engagement soon.

Kandy and her fiancé did come to see me and I took them on as clients. They are progressing well but Kandy is a real pistol. I can see a good story about her in the future.

I also see the security guard and his wife. She wears the pants in the family and bosses him around. He immediately found another job after the state retired him so he could avoid being with her. After a few sessions, they started talking again and even went on a vacation, something they haven't done in twenty years. He quit the new job to be at home more. The relationship has a long way to go but I'm positive about it.

Susan wants me to write another book, and maybe I will someday, but not in the near future. My life is back to normal and I'm happy being a marriage counselor. My father has always said that helping couples stay together was a great job and personally rewarding. It is and I'm working hard to be better at it.

I'm sure you're wondering if I still use the test. I do, but I don't talk about it anymore. If you have any rules you think I should include, send me an email. I'm always looking for ways to improve it.

The end.

35115750R00095

Made in the USA
Middletown, DE
19 September 2016